James Blish

The Thing in the Attic & Other Stories by James Blish

e-artnow 2020

James Blish
The Thing in the Attic & Other Stories by James Blish

To Pay the Piper, One-Shot

e-artnow, 2020
Contact: info@e-artnow.org

ISBN 978-80-273-0908-5

Contents

The Thing in the Attic   11

To Pay the Piper   30

One-Shot   40

The Thing in the Attic

It is written that after the Giants came to Tellura from the far stars, they abode a while, and looked upon the surface of the land, and found it wanting, and of evil omen. Therefore did they make men to live always in the air and in the sunlight, and in the light of the stars, that he would be reminded of them. And the Giants abode yet a while, and taught men to speak, and to write, and to weave, and to do many things which are needful to do, of which the writings speak. And thereafter they departed to the far stars, saying, Take this world as your own, and though we shall return, fear not, for it is yours.
—THE BOOK OF LAWS

Honath and his fellow arch-doubters did not believe in the Giants, and for this they were cast into Hell. And when survival depended upon unwavering faith in their beliefs, they saw that there were Giants, after all....

Honath the Pursemaker was hauled from the nets an hour before the rest of the prisoners, as befitted his role as the arch-doubter of them all. It was not yet dawn, but his captors led him in great bounds through the endless, musky-perfumed orchid gardens, small dark shapes with crooked legs, hunched shoulders, slim hairless tails carried, like his, in concentric spirals wound clockwise. Behind them sprang Honath on the end of a long tether, timing his leaps by theirs, since any slip would hang him summarily.

He would of course be on his way to the surface, some 250 feet below the orchid gardens, shortly after dawn in any event. But not even the arch-doubter of them all wanted to begin the trip-not even at the merciful snap-spine end of a tether —a moment before the law said, Go.

The looping, interwoven network of vines beneath them, each cable as thick through as a man's body, bellied out and down sharply as the leapers reached the edge of the fern-tree forest which surrounded the copse of fan-palms. The whole party stopped before beginning the descent and looked eastward, across the dim bowl. The stars were paling more and more rapidly; only the bright constellation of the Parrot could still be picked out without doubt.

"A fine day," one of the guards said, conversationally. "Better to go below on a sunny day than in the rain, pursemaker."

Honath shuddered and said nothing. Of course it was always raining down below in Hell, that much could be seen by a child. Even on sunny days, the endless pinpoint rain of transpiration, from the hundred million leaves of the eternal trees, hazed the forest air and soaked the black bog forever.

He looked around in the brightening, misty morning. The eastern horizon was black against the limb of the great red sun, which had already risen about a third of its diameter; it was almost time for the small, blue-white, furiously hot consort to follow. All the way to that brink, as to every other horizon, the woven ocean of the treetops flowed gently in long, unbreaking waves, featureless as some smooth oil. Only nearby could the eye break that ocean into its details, into the world as it was: a great, many-tiered network, thickly overgrown with small ferns, with air-drinking orchids, with a thousand varieties of fungi sprouting wherever vine crossed vine and collected a little humus for them, with the vivid parasites sucking sap from the vines, the trees, and even each other. In the ponds of rain-water collected by the closely fitting leaves of the bromeliads tree-toads and peepers stopped down their hoarse songs dubiously as the light grew and fell silent one by one. In the trees below the world, the tentative morning screeches of the lizard-birds —the souls of the damned, or the devils who hunted them, no one was quite sure which-took up the concert.

A small gust of wind whipped out of the hollow above the glade of fan-palms, making the network under the party shift slightly, as if in a loom. Honath gave with it easily, automatically, but one of the smaller vines toward which he had moved one furless hand hissed at him and went pouring away into the darkness beneath —a chlorophyll-green snake, come up out of the dripping aerial pathways in which it hunted in ancestral gloom, to greet the suns and dry its scales in the quiet morning. Farther below, an astonished monkey, routed out of its bed by the disgusted serpent, sprang into another tree, reeling off ten mortal insults, one after the other, while still in mid-leap. The snake, of course, paid no attention, since it did not speak the language of men; but the party on the edge of the glade of fan-palms snickered appreciatively.

"Bad language they favor below," another of the guards said. "A fit place for you and your blasphemers, pursemaker. Come now."

The tether at Honath's neck twitched, and then his captors were soaring in zig-zag bounds down into the hollow toward the Judgment Seat. He followed, since he had no choice, the tether threatening constantly to foul his arms, legs or tail, and-worse, far worse-making his every mortifying movement ungraceful. Above, the Parrot's starry plumes flickered and faded into the general blue.

Toward the center of the saucer above the grove, the stitched leaf-and-leather houses clustered thickly, bound to the vines themselves, or hanging from an occasional branch too high or too slender to bear the vines. Many of these purses Honath knew well, not only as visitor but as artisan. The finest of them, the inverted flowers which opened automatically as the morning dew bathed them, yet which could be closed tightly and safely around their occupants at dusk by a single draw-string, were his own design as well as his own handiwork. They had been widely admired and imitated.

The reputation that they had given him, too, had helped to bring him to the end of the snap-spine tether. They had given weight to his words among others-weight enough to make him, at last, the arch-doubter, the man who leads the young into blasphemy, the man who questions the Book of Laws.

And they had probably helped to win him his passage on the Elevator to Hell.

The purses were already opening as the party swung among them. Here and there, sleepy faces blinked out from amid the exfoliating sections, criss-crossed by relaxing lengths of dew-soaked rawhide. Some of the awakening householders recognized Honath, of that he was sure, but none came out to follow the party-though the villagers should be beginning to drop from the hearts of their stitched flowers like ripe seed-pods by this hour of any normal day.

A Judgment was at hand, and they knew it-and even those who had slept the night in one of Honath's finest houses would not speak for him now. Everyone knew, after all, that Honath did not believe in the Giants.

Honath could see the Judgment Seat itself now, a slung chair of woven cane crowned along the back with a row of gigantic mottled orchids. These had supposedly been transplanted there when the chair was made, but no one could remember how old they were; since there were no seasons, there was no particular reason why they should not have been there forever. The Seat itself was at the back of the arena and high above it, but in the gathering light Honath could make out the white-furred face of the Tribal Spokesman, like a lone silver-and-black pansy among the huge vivid blooms.

At the center of the arena proper was the Elevator itself. Honath had seen it often enough, and had himself witnessed Judgments where it was called into use, but he could still hardly believe that he was almost surely to be its next passenger. It consisted of nothing more than a large basket, deep enough so that one would have to leap out of it, and rimmed with thorns to prevent one from leaping back in. Three hempen ropes were tied to its rim, and were then cunningly interwound on a single-drum windlass of wood, which could be turned by two men even when the basket was loaded.

The procedure was equally simple. The condemned man was forced into the basket, and the basket lowered out of sight, until the slackening of the ropes indicated that it had touched the surface. The victim climbed out-and if he did not, the basket remained below until he starved or until Hell otherwise took care of its own-and the windlass was rewound.

The sentences were for varying periods of time, according to the severity of the crime, but in practical terms this formality was empty. Although the basket was dutifully lowered when the sentence had expired, no one had ever been known to get back into it. Of course, in a world without seasons or moons, and hence without any but an arbitrary year, long periods of time are not easy to count accurately. The basket could arrive thirty or forty days to one side or the other of the proper date. But this was only a technicality, however, for if keeping time was difficult in the attic world it was probably impossible in Hell.

Honath's guards tied the free end of his tether to a branch and settled down around him. One abstractedly passed a pine cone to him and he tried to occupy his mind with the business of picking the juicy seeds from it, but somehow they had no flavor.

More captives were being brought in now, while the Spokesman watched with glittering black eyes from his high perch. There was Mathild the Forager, shivering as if with ague, the fur down her left side glistening and spiky, as though she had inadvertently overturned a tank plant on herself. After her was brought Alaskon the Navigator, a middle-aged man only a few years younger than Honath himself; he was tied up next to Honath, where he settled down at once, chewing at a joint of cane with apparent indifference.

Thus far, the gathering had proceeded without more than a few words being spoken, but that ended when the guards tried to bring Seth the Needlesmith from the nets. He could be heard at once, over the entire distance to the glade, alternately chattering and shrieking in a mixture of tones that might mean either fear or fury. Everyone in the glade but Alaskon turned to look, and heads emerged from purses like new butterflies from cocoons.

A moment later, Seth's guards came over the lip of the glade in a tangled group, now shouting themselves. Somewhere in the middle of the knot Seth's voice became still louder; obviously he was clinging with all five members to any vine or frond he could grasp, and was no sooner pried loose from one than he would leap by main force, backwards if possible, to another. Nevertheless he was being brought inexorably down into the arena, two feet forward, one foot back, three feet forward....

Honath's guards resumed picking their pine-cones. During the disturbance, Honath realized Charl the Reader had been brought in quietly from the same side of the glade. He now sat opposite Alaskon, looking apathetically down at the vine-web, his shoulders hunched forward. He exuded despair; even to look at him made Honath feel a renewed shudder.

From the High Seat, the Spokesman said: "Honath the Pursemaker, Alaskon the Navigator, Charl the Reader, Seth the Needlesmith Mathild the Forager, you are called to answer to justice."

"Justice!" Seth shouted, springing free of his captors with a tremendous bound and bringing up with a jerk on the end of his tether. "This is no justice! I have nothing to do with —"

The guards caught up with him and clamped brown hands firmly over his mouth. The Spokesman watched with amused malice.

"The accusations are three," the Spokesman said. "The first, the telling of lies to children. Second, the casting into doubt of the divine order among men. Third, the denial of the Book of Laws. Each of you may speak in order of age. Honath the Pursemaker, your plea may be heard."

Honath stood up, trembling a little, but feeling a surprisingly renewed surge of his old independence.

"Your charges," he said, "all rest upon the denial of the Book of Laws. I have taught nothing else that is contrary to what we all believe, and called nothing else into doubt. And I deny the charge."

The Spokesman looked down at him with disbelief. "Many men and women have said that you do not believe in the Giants, pursemaker," he said. "You will not win mercy by piling up more lies."

"I deny the charge," Honath insisted. "I believe in the Book of Laws as a whole, and I believe in the Giants. I have taught only that the Giants were not real in the sense that we are real. I have taught that they were intended as symbols of some higher reality and were not meant to be taken as literal persons."

"What higher reality is this?" the Spokesman demanded. "Describe it."

"You ask me to do something the writers of the Book of Laws themselves couldn't do," Honath said hotly. "If they had to embody the reality in symbols rather than writing it down directly, how could a mere pursemaker do better?"

"This doctrine is wind," the Spokesman said. "And it is plainly intended to undercut authority and the order established by the Book. Tell me, pursemaker: if men need not fear the Giants, why should they fear the law?"

"Because they are men, and it is to their interest to fear the law. They aren't children, who need some physical Giant sitting over them with a whip to make them behave. Furthermore, Spokesman, this archaic belief *itself* undermines us. As long as we believe that there are real Giants, and that some day they'll return and resume teaching us, so long will we fail to seek answers to our questions for ourselves. Half of what we know was given to us in the Book, and the other half is supposed to drop to us from the skies if we wait long enough. In the meantime, we vegetate."

"If a part of the Book be untrue, there can be nothing to prevent that it is all untrue," the Spokesman said heavily. "And we will lose even what you call the half of our knowledge-which is actually the whole of it-to those who see with clear eyes."

Suddenly, Honath lost his temper. "Lose it, then!" he shouted. "Let us unlearn everything we know only by rote, go back to the beginning, learn all over again, and *continue* to learn, from our own experience. Spokesman, you are an old man, but there are still some of us who haven't forgotten what curiosity means!"

"Quiet!" the Spokesman said. "We have heard enough. We call on Alaskon the Navigator."

"Much of the Book is clearly untrue," Alaskon said flatly, rising. "As a handbook of small trades it has served us well. As a guide to how the universe is made, it is nonsense, in my opinion; Honath is too kind to it. I've made no secret of what I think, and I still think it."

"And will pay for it," the Spokesman said, blinking slowly down at Alaskon. "Charl the Reader."

"Nothing," Charl said, without standing, or even looking up.

"You do not deny the charges?"

"I've nothing to say," Charl said, but then, abruptly, his head jerked up, and he glared with desperate eyes at the Spokesman. "I can read, Spokesman. I have seen words in the Book of Laws that contradict each other. I've pointed them out. They're facts, they exist on the pages. I've taught nothing, told no lies, preached no unbelief. I've pointed to the facts. That's all."

"Seth the Needlesmith, you may speak now."

The guards took their hands gratefully off Seth's mouth; they had been bitten several times in the process of keeping him quiet up to now. Seth resumed shouting at once.

"I'm no part of this group! I'm the victim of gossip, envious neighbors, smiths jealous of my skill and my custom! No man can say worse of me than that I sold needles to this pursemaker-sold them in good faith! The charges against me are lies, all lies!"

Honath jumped to his feet in fury, and then sat down again, choking back the answering shout almost without tasting its bitterness. What did it matter? Why should he bear witness against the young man? It would not help the others, and if Seth wanted to lie his way out of Hell, he might as well be given the chance.

The Spokesman was looking down at Seth with the identical expression of outraged disbelief which he had first bent upon Honath. "Who was it cut the blasphemies into the hardwood tree, by the house of Hosi the Lawgiver?" he demanded. "Sharp needles were at work there, and there are witnesses to say that your hands held them."

"More lies!"

"Needles found in your house fit the furrows, Seth."

"They were not mine-or they were stolen! I demand to be freed!"

"You will be freed," the Spokesman said coldly. There was no possible doubt as to what he meant. Seth began to weep and to shout at the same time. Hands closed over his mouth again. "Mathild the Forager, your plea may be heard."

The young woman stood up hesitantly. Her fur was nearly dry now, but she was still shivering.

"Spokesman," she said, "I saw the things which Charl the Reader showed me. I doubted, but what Honath said restored my belief. I see no harm in his teachings. They remove doubt, instead of fostering it as you say they do. I see no evil in them, and I don't understand why this is a crime."

Honath looked over to her with new admiration. The Spokesman sighed heavily.

"I am sorry for you," he said, "but as Spokesman we cannot allow ignorance of the law as a plea. We will be merciful to you all, however. Renounce your heresy, affirm your belief in the Book as it is written from bark to bark, and you shall be no more than cast out of the tribe."

"I renounce it!" Seth cried. "I never shared it! It's all blasphemy and every word is a lie! I believe in the Book, all of it!"

"You, needlesmith," the Spokesman said, "have lied before this Judgment, and are probably lying now. You are not included in the dispensation."

"Snake-spotted caterpillar! May your —*ummulph.*"

"Pursemaker, what is your answer?"

"It is No," Honath said stonily. "I've spoken the truth. The truth can't be unsaid."

The Spokesman looked down at the rest of them. "As for you three, consider your answers carefully. To share the heresy means sharing the sentence. The penalty will not be lightened only because you did not invent the heresy."

There was a long silence.

Honath swallowed hard. The courage and the faith in that silence made him feel smaller and more helpless than ever. He realized suddenly that the other three would have kept that silence, even without Seth's defection to stiffen their spines. He wondered if he could have done so.

"Then we pronounce the sentence," the Spokesman said. "You are one and all condemned to one thousand days in Hell."

There was a concerted gasp from around the edges of the arena, where, without Honath's having noticed it before, a silent crowd had gathered. He did not wonder at the sound. The sentence was the longest in the history of the tribe.

Not that it really meant anything. No one had ever come back from as little as one hundred days in Hell. No one had ever come back from Hell at all.

"Unlash the Elevator. All shall go together."

———————————————

The basket swayed. The last of the attic world that Honath saw was a circle of faces, not too close to the gap in the vine web, peering down after them. Then the basket fell another few yards to the next turn of the windlass and the faces vanished.

Seth was weeping in the bottom of the Elevator, curled up into a tight ball, the end of his tail wrapped around his nose and eyes. No one else could make a sound, least of Honath.

The gloom closed around them. It seemed extraordinarily still. The occasional harsh screams of a lizard-bird somehow distended the silence without breaking it. The light that filtered down into the long aisles between the trees seemed to be absorbed in a blue-green haze through which the lianas wove their long curved lines. The columns of tree-trunks, the pillars of the world, stood all around them, too distant in the dim light to allow them to gauge their speed of descent.

15

Only the irregular plunges of the basket proved that it was even in motion any longer, though it swayed laterally in a complex, overlapping series of figure-eights.

Then the basket lurched downward once more, brought up short, and tipped sidewise, tumbling them all against the hard cane. Mathild cried out in a thin voice, and Seth uncurled almost instantly, clawing for a handhold. Another lurch, and the Elevator lay down on its side and was still.

They were in Hell.

Cautiously, Honath began to climb out, picking his way over the long thorns on the basket's rim. After a moment, Charl the Reader followed, and then Alaskon took Mathild firmly by the hand and led her out onto the surface. The footing was wet and spongy, yet not at all resilient, and it felt cold; Honath's toes curled involuntarily.

"Come on, Seth," Charl said in a hushed voice. "They won't haul it back up until we're all out. You know that."

Alaskon looked around into the chilly mists. "Yes," he said. "And we'll need a needlesmith down here. With good tools, there's just a chance —"

Seth's eyes had been darting back and forth from one to the other. With a sudden chattering scream, he bounded out of the bottom of the basket, soaring over their heads in a long, flat leap and struck the high knee at the base of the nearest tree, an immense fan palm. As he hit, his legs doubled under him, and almost in the same motion he seemed to rocket straight up into the murky air.

Gaping, Honath looked up after him. The young needlesmith had timed his course to the split second. He was already darting up the rope from which the Elevator was suspended. He did not even bother to look back.

After a moment, the basket tipped upright. The impact of Seth's weight hitting the rope evidently had been taken by the windlass team to mean that the condemned people were all out on the surface; a twitch on the rope was the usual signal. The basket began to rise, hobbling and dancing. Its speed of ascent, added to Seth's took his racing, dwindling figure out of sight quickly. After a while, the basket was gone, too.

"He'll never get to the top," Mathild whispered. "It's too far, and he's going too fast. He'll lose strength and fall."

"I don't think so," Alaskon said heavily. "He's agile and strong. If anyone could make it, he could."

"They'll kill him if he does."

"Of course they will," Alaskon said, shrugging.

"I won't miss him," Honath said.

"No more will I. But we could use some sharp needles down here, Honath. Now we'll have to plan to make our own-if we can identify the different woods, down here where there aren't any leaves to help us tell them apart."

Honath looked at the navigator curiously. Seth's bolt for the sky had distracted him from the realization that the basket, too, was gone, but now that desolate fact hit home. "You actually plan to stay alive in Hell, don't you, Alaskon?"

"Certainly," Alaskon said calmly. "This is no more Hell than-up there-is Heaven. It's the surface of the planet, no more, no less. We can stay alive if we don't panic. Were you just going to sit here until the furies came for you, Honath?"

"I hadn't thought much about it," Honath confessed. "But if there is any chance that Seth will lose his grip on that rope-before he reaches the top and they stab him-shouldn't we wait and see if we can catch him? He can't weigh more than 35 pounds. Maybe we could contrive some sort of a net —"

"He'd just break our bones along with his," Charl said. "I'm for getting out of here as fast as possible."

"What for? Do you know a better place?"

"No, but whether this is Hell or not, there are demons down here. We've all seen them from up above. They must know that the Elevator always lands here and empties out free food. This must be a feeding-ground for them —"

He had not quite finished speaking when the branches began to sigh and toss, far above. A gust of stinging droplets poured along the blue air and thunder rumbled. Mathild whimpered.

"It's only a squall coming up," Honath said. But the words came out in a series of short croaks. As the wind had moved through the trees, Honath had automatically flexed his knees and put his arms out for handholds, awaiting the long wave of response to pass through the ground beneath him. But nothing happened. The surface under his feet remained stolidly where it was, flexing not a fraction of an inch in any direction. And there was nothing nearby for his hands to grasp.

He staggered, trying to compensate for the failure of the ground to move. At the same moment another gust of wind blew through the aisles, a little stronger than the first, and calling insistently for a new adjustment of his body to the waves which would be passing among the treetops. Again the squashy surface beneath him refused to respond. The familiar give-and-take of the vine-web to the winds, a part of his world as accustomed as the winds themselves, was gone.

Honath was forced to sit down, feeling distinctly ill. The damp, cool earth under his furless buttocks was unpleasant, but he could not have remained standing any longer without losing his meagre prisoner's breakfast. One grappling hand caught hold of the ridged, gritting stems of a clump of horsetail, but the contact failed to allay the uneasiness.

The others seemed to be bearing it no better than Honath. Mathild in particular was rocking dizzily, her lips compressed, her hands clasped to her delicate ears.

Dizziness. It was unheard of up above, except among those who had suffered grave head injuries or were otherwise very ill. But on the motionless ground of Hell, it was evidently going to be with them constantly.

Charl squatted, swallowing convulsively. "I —I can't stand," he moaned.

"Nonsense!" Alaskon said, though he had remained standing only by clinging to the huge, mud-colored bulb of a cycadella. "It's just a disturbance of our sense of balance. We'll get used to it."

"We'd better," Honath said, relinquishing his grip on the horsetails by a sheer act of will. "I think Charl's right about this being a feeding-ground, Alaskon. I hear something moving around in the ferns. And if this rain lasts long, the water will rise here, too. I've seen silver flashes from down here many a time after heavy rains."

"That's right," Mathild said, her voice subdued. "The base of the fan-palm grove always floods. That's why the treetops are lower there."

The wind seemed to have let up a little, though the rain was still falling. Alaskon stood up tentatively and looked around.

"Then let's move on," he said. "If we try to keep under cover until we get to higher ground —"

A faint crackling sound, high above his head, interrupted him. It got louder. Feeling a sudden spasm of pure fear, Honath looked up.

Nothing could be seen for an instant but the far-away curtain of branches and fern fronds. Then, with shocking suddenness, something plummeted through the blue-green roof and came tumbling toward them. It was a man, twisting and tumbling through the air with grotesque slowness, like a child turning in its sleep. They scattered.

The body hit the ground with a sodden thump, but there were sharp overtones to the sound, like the bursting of a gourd. For a moment nobody moved. Then Honath crept forward.

It had been Seth, as Honath had realized the moment the figurine had burst through the branches far above. But it had not been the fall that had killed him. He had been run through by at least a dozen needles-some of them, beyond doubt, tools from his own shop, their points edged hair-fine by his own precious strops of leatherwood-bark.

There would be no reprieve from above. The sentence was one thousand days. This burst and broken huddle of fur was the only alternative.

And the first day had barely begun.

They toiled all the rest of the day to reach higher ground. As they stole cautiously closer to the foothills of the Great Range and the ground became firmer, they were able to take to the air for short stretches, but they were no sooner aloft among the willows than the lizard-birds came squalling down on them by the dozens, fighting among each other for the privilege of nipping these plump and incredibly slow-moving monkeys.

No man, no matter how confirmed a free-thinker, could have stood up under such an on-slaught by the creatures he had been taught as a child to think of as his ancestors. The first time it happened, every member of the party dropped like a pine-cone to the sandy ground and lay paralyzed under the nearest cover, until the brindle-feathered, fan-tailed screamers tired of flying in such tight circles and headed for clearer air. Even after the lizard-birds had given up, they crouched quietly for a long time, waiting to see what greater demons might have been attracted by the commotion.

Luckily, on the higher ground there was much more cover from low-growing shrubs and trees-palmetto, sassafras, several kinds of laurel, magnolia, and a great many sedges. Up here, too, the endless jungle began to break around the bases of the great pink cliffs. Overhead were welcome vistas of open sky, sketchily crossed by woven bridges leading from the vine-world to the cliffs themselves. In the intervening columns of blue air a whole hierarchy of flying creatures ranked themselves, layer by layer. First, the low-flying beetles, bees and two-winged insects. Next were the dragonflies which hunted them, some with wingspreads as wide as two feet. Then the lizard-birds, hunting the dragonflies and anything else that could he nipped without fighting back. And at last, far above, the great gliding reptiles coasting along the brows of the cliffs, riding the rising currents of air, their long-jawed hunger stalking anything that flew-as they sometimes stalked the birds of the attic world, and the flying fish along the breast of the distant sea.

The party halted in an especially thick clump of sedges. Though the rain continued to fall, harder than ever, they were all desperately thirsty. They had yet to find a single bromelaid: evidently the tank-plants did not grow in Hell. Cupping their hands to the weeping sky accu-mulated surprisingly little water; and no puddles large enough to drink from accumulated on the sand. But at least, here under the open sky, there was too much fierce struggle in the air to allow the lizard-birds to congregate and squall about their hiding place.

The white sun had already set and the red sun's vast arc still bulged above the horizon. In the lurid glow the rain looked like blood, and the seamed faces of the pink cliffs had all but vanished. Honath peered dubiously out from under the sedges at the still distant escarpments.

"I don't see how we can hope to climb those," he said, in a low voice. "That kind of limestone crumbles as soon as you touch it, otherwise we'd have had better luck with our war against the cliff tribe."

"We could go around the cliffs," Charl said. "The foothills of the Great Range aren't very steep. If we could last until we get to them, we could go on up into the Range itself."

"To the volcanoes!" Mathild protested. "But nothing can live up there, nothing but the white fire-things. And there are the lava-flows, too, and the choking smoke —"

"Well, we can't climb these cliffs. Honath's quite right," Alaskon said. "And we can't climb the Basalt Steppes, either-there's nothing to eat along them, let alone any water or cover. I don't see what else we can do but try to get up into the foothills."

"Can't we stay here?" Mathild said plaintively.

"No," Honath said, even more gently than he had intended. Mathild's four words were, he knew, the most dangerous words in Hell-he knew it quite surely, because of the imprisoned creature inside him that cried out to say "Yes" instead. "We have to get out of the country of the demons. And maybe-just maybe-if we can cross the Great Range, we can join a tribe that hasn't heard about our being condemned to Hell. There are supposed to be tribes on the other side of the Range, but the cliff people would never let our folk get through to them. That's on our side now."

"That's true," Alaskon said, brightening a little. "And from the top of the Range, we could come *down* into another tribe-instead of trying to climb up into their village out of Hell. Honath, I think it might work."

"Then we'd better try to sleep right here and now," Charl said. "It seems safe enough. If we're going to skirt the cliffs and climb those foothills, we'll need all the strength we've got left."

Honath was about to protest, but he was suddenly too tired to care. Why not sleep it over? And if in the night they were found and taken-well, that would at least put an end to the struggle.

It was a cheerless and bone-damp bed to sleep in, but there was no alternative. They curled up as best they could. Just before he was about to drop off at last, Honath heard Mathild whimpering to herself and, on impulse, crawled over to her and began to smooth down her fur with his tongue. To his astonishment each separate, silky hair was loaded with dew. Long before the girl had curled herself more tightly and her complaints had dwindled into sleepy murmurs, Honath's thirst was assuaged. He reminded himself to mention the method in the morning.

But when the white sun finally came up, there was no time to think of thirst. Charl the Reader was gone. Something had plucked him from their huddled midst as neatly as a fallen breadfruit-and had dropped his cleaned ivory skull just as negligently, some two hundred feet farther on up the slope which led toward the pink cliffs.

Late that afternoon, the three found the blue, turbulent stream flowing out of the foothills of the Great Range. Not even Alaskon knew quite what to make of it. It looked like water, but it flowed like the rivers of lava that crept downward from the volcanoes. Whatever else it could be, obviously it wasn't water; water stood, it never flowed. It was possible to imagine a still body of water as big as this, but only in a moment of fancy, an exaggeration derived from the known bodies of water in the tank-plants. But this much water in motion? It suggested pythons; it was probably poisonous. It did not occur to any of them to drink from it. They were afraid even to touch it, let alone cross it, for it was almost surely as hot as the other kinds of lava-rivers. They followed its course cautiously into the foothills, their throats as dry and gritty as the hollow stems of horsetails.

Except for the thirst-which was in an inverted sense their friend, insofar as it overrode the hunger-the climbing was not difficult. It was only circuitous, because of the need to stay under cover, to reconnoiter every few yards, to choose the most sheltered course rather than the most direct. By an unspoken consent, none of the three mentioned Charl, but their eyes were constantly darting from side to side, searching for a glimpse of the thing that had taken him.

That was perhaps the worst, the most terrifying part of the tragedy: not once, since they had been in Hell, had they actually seen a demon-or even any animal as large as a man. The enormous, three-taloned footprint they had found in the sand beside their previous night's bed-the spot where the thing had stood, looking down at the four sleepers from above, coldly deciding which of them to seize-was the only evidence they had that they were now really in the same world with the demons. The world of the demons they had sometimes looked down upon from the remote vine-webs.

The footprint-and the skull.

By nightfall, they had ascended perhaps a hundred and fifty feet. It was difficult to judge distances in the twilight, and the token vine bridges from the attic world to the pink cliffs were now cut off from sight by the intervening masses of the cliffs themselves. But there was no possibility that they could climb higher today. Although Mathild had born the climb surprisingly well, and Honath himself still felt almost fresh, Alaskon was completely winded. He had taken a bad cut on one hip from a serrated spike of volcanic glass against which he had stumbled. The wound, bound with leaves to prevent its leaving a spoor which might be followed, evidently was becoming steadily more painful.

Honath finally called a halt as soon as they reached the little ridge with the cave in back of it. Helping Alaskon over the last boulders, he was astonished to discover how hot the navigator's hands were. He took him back into the cave and then came out onto the ledge again.

"He's really sick," he told Mathild in a low voice. "He needs water, and another dressing for that cut. And we've got to get both for him somehow. If we ever get to the jungle on the other side of the Range, we'll need a navigator even worse than we need a needlesmith."

"But how? I could dress the cut if I had the materials, Honath. But there's no water up here. It's a desert; we'll never get across it."

"We've got to try. I can get him water, I think. There was a big cycladella on the slope we came up, just before we passed that obsidian spur that hurt Alaskon. Gourds that size usually have a fair amount of water inside them and I can use a piece of the spur to rip it open —"

A small hand came out of the darkness and took him tightly by the elbow. "Honath, you can't go back down there. Suppose the demon that-that took Charl is still following us? They hunt at night-and this country is all so strange...."

"I can find my way. I'll follow the sound of the stream of blue lava or whatever it is. You pull some fresh leaves for Alaskon and try to make him comfortable. Better loosen those vines around the dressing a little. I'll be back."

He touched her hand and pried it loose gently. Then, without stopping to think about it any further, he slipped off the ledge and edged toward the sound of the stream, travelling crabwise on all fours.

But he was swiftly lost. The night was thick and completely impenetrable, and he found that the noise of the stream seemed to come from all sides, providing him no guide at all. Furthermore, his memory of the ridge which led up to the cave appeared to be faulty, for he could feel it turning sharply to the right beneath him, though he remembered distinctly that it had been straight past the first side-branch, and then had gone to the left. Or had he passed the first side-branch in the dark without seeing it? He probed the darkness cautiously with one hand.

At the same instant, a brisk, staccato gust of wind came whirling up out of the night across the ridge. Instinctively, Honath shifted his weight to take up the flexing of the ground beneath him.

He realized his error instantly and tried to arrest the complex set of motions, but a habit-pattern so deeply ingrained could not be frustrated completely. Overwhelmed with vertigo, Honath grappled at the empty air with hands, feet and tail and went toppling.

An instant later, with a familiar noise and an equally familiar cold shock that seemed to reach throughout his body, he was sitting in the midst of —

Water. Icy water. Water that rushed by him improbably with a menacing, monkeylike chattering, but water all the same.

It was all he could do to repress a hoot of hysteria. He hunkered down into the stream and soaked himself. Things nibbled delicately at his calves as he bathed, but he had no reason to fear fish, small species of which often showed up in the tanks of the bromelaids. After lowering his muzzle to the rushing, invisible surface and drinking his fill, he dunked himself completely and then clambered out onto the banks, carefully neglecting to shake himself.

Getting back to the ledge was much less difficult. "Mathild?" he called in a hoarse whisper. "Mathild, we've got water."

"Come in here quick then. Alaskon's worse. I'm afraid, Honath."

Dripping, Honath felt his way into the cave. "I don't have any container. I just got myself wet-you'll have to sit him up and let him lick my fur."

"I'm not sure he can."

But Alaskon could, feebly, but sufficiently. Even the coldness of the water —a totally new experience for a man who had never drunk anything but the soup-warm contents of the brome-laids-seemed to help him. He lay back at last, and said in a weak but otherwise normal voice: "So the stream was water after all."

"Yes," Honath said. "And there are fish in it, too."

"Don't talk," Mathild said. "Rest, Alaskon."

"I'm resting. Honath, if we stick to the course of the stream.... Where was I? Oh. We can follow the stream through the Range, now that we know it's water. How did you find that out?"

"I lost my balance and fell into it."

Alaskon chuckled. "Hell's not so bad, is it?" he said. Then he sighed, and rushes creaked under him.

"Mathild! What's the matter? Is he-did he die?"

"No ...no. He's breathing. He's still sicker than he realizes, that's all.... Honath-if they'd known, up above, how much courage you have —"

"I was scared white," Honath said grimly. "I'm still scared."

But her hand touched his again in the solid blackness, and after he had taken it, he felt irrationally cheerful. With Alaskon breathing so raggedly behind them, there was little chance that either of them would be able to sleep that night; but they sat silently together on the hard stone in a kind of temporary peace. When the mouth of the cave began to outline itself with the first glow of the red sun, they looked at each other in a conspiracy of light all their own.

Let us unlearn everything we knew only by rote, go back to the beginning, learn all over again, and continue to learn....

With the first light of the white sun, a half-grown megatherium cub rose slowly from its crouch at the mouth of the cave and stretched luxuriously, showing a full set of saber-like teeth. It looked at them steadily for a moment, its ears alert, then turned and loped away down the slope.

How long it had been crouched there listening to them, it was impossible to know. They had been lucky that they had stumbled into the lair of a youngster. A full-grown animal would have killed them all, within a few seconds after its cat's-eyes had collected enough dawn to identify them positively. The cub, since it had no family of its own, evidently had only been puzzled to find its den occupied and didn't want to quarrel about it.

The departure of the big cat left Honath frozen, not so much frightened as simply stunned by so unexpected an end to the vigil. At the first moan from Alaskon, however, Mathild was up and walking softly to the navigator, speaking in a low voice, sentences which made no particular sense and perhaps were not intended to. Honath stirred and followed her.

Halfway back into the cave, his foot struck something and he looked down. It was the thigh-bone of some medium-large animal, imperfectly cleaned and not very recent. It looked like a keepsake the megatherium had hoped to save from the usurpers of its lair. Along a curved inner surface there was a patch of thick grey mold. Honath squatted and peeled it off carefully.

"Mathild, we can put this over the wound," he said. "Some molds help prevent wounds from festering.... How is he?"

"Better, I think," Mathild murmured. "But he's still feverish. I don't think we'll be able to move on today."

Honath was unsure whether to be pleased or disturbed. Certainly he was far from anxious to leave the cave, where they seemed at least to be reasonably comfortable. Possibly they would also be reasonably safe, for the low-roofed hole almost surely still smelt of megatherium, and intruders would recognize the smell-as the men from the attic world could not-and keep their distance. They would have no way of knowing that the cat had only been a cub and that it had vacated the premises, though of course the odor would fade before long.

Yet it was important to move on, to cross the Great Range if possible, and in the end to wind their way back to the world where they belonged. And to win vindication, no matter how long it took. Even should it prove relatively easy to survive in Hell-and there were few signs of that, thus far-the only proper course was to fight until the attic world was totally regained. After all, it would have been the easy and the comfortable thing, back there at the very beginning, to have kept one's incipient heresies to oneself and remained on comfortable terms with one's neighbors. But Honath had spoken up, and so had the rest of them, in their fashions.

It was the ancient internal battle between what Honath wanted to do, and what he knew he ought to do. He had never heard of Kant and the Categorical Imperative, but he knew well enough which side of his nature would win in the long run. But it had been a cruel joke of heredity which had fastened a sense of duty onto a lazy nature. It made even small decisions egregiously painful.

But for the moment at least, the decision was out of his hands. Alaskon was too sick to be moved. In addition, the strong beams of sunlight which had been glaring in across the floor of the cave were dimming by the instant, and there was a distant, premonitory growl of thunder.

"Then we'll stay here," he said. "It's going to rain again, and hard this time. Once it's falling in earnest, I can go out and pick us some fruit-it'll screen me even if anything is prowling around in it. And I won't have to go as far as the stream for water, as long as the rain keeps up."

The rain, as it turned out, kept up all day, in a growing downpour which completely curtained the mouth of the cave by early afternoon. The chattering of the nearby stream grew quickly to a roar.

By evening, Alaskon's fever seemed to have dropped almost to normal, and his strength nearly returned as well. The wound, thanks more to the encrusted matte of mold than to any complications within the flesh itself, was still ugly-looking, but it was now painful only when the navigator moved carelessly, and Mathild was convinced that it was mending. Alaskon himself, having been deprived of activity all day, was unusually talkative.

"Has it occurred to either of you," he said in the gathering gloom, "that since that stream is water, it can't possibly be coming from the Great Range? All the peaks over there are just cones of ashes and lava. We've seen young volcanoes in the process of building themselves, so we're sure of that. What's more, they're usually hot. I don't see how there could possibly be any source of water in the Range-not even run-off from the rains."

"It can't just come up out of the ground," Honath said. "It must be fed by rain. By the way it sounds now, it could even be the first part of a flood."

"As you say, it's probably rain-water," Alaskon said cheerfully. "But not off the Great Range, that's out of the question. Most likely it collects on the cliffs."

"I hope you're wrong," Honath said. "The cliffs may be a little easier to climb from this side, but there's still the cliff tribe to think about."

"Maybe, maybe. But the cliffs are big. The tribes on this side may never have heard of the war with our tree-top folk. No, Honath, I think that's our only course."

"If it is," Honath said grimly, "we're going to wish more than ever that we had some stout, sharp needles among us."

Alaskon's judgment was quickly borne out. The three left the cave at dawn the next morning, Alaskon moving somewhat stiffly but not otherwise noticeably incommoded, and resumed following the stream bed upwards —a stream now swollen by the rains to a roaring rapids. After winding its way upwards for about a mile in the general direction of the Great Range, the stream turned on itself and climbed rapidly back toward the basalt cliffs, falling toward the three over successively steeper shelves of jutting rock.

Then it turned again, at right angles, and the three found themselves at the exit of a dark gorge, little more than thirty feet high, but both narrow and long. Here the stream was almost perfectly smooth, and the thin strip of land on each side of it was covered with low shrubs. They paused and looked dubiously into the canyon. It was singularly gloomy.

"There's plenty of cover, at least," Honath said in a low voice. "But almost anything could live in a place like that."

"Nothing very big could hide in it," Alaskon pointed out. "It should be safe. Anyhow it's the only way to go."

"All right. Let's go ahead, then. But keep your head down, and be ready to jump!"

Honath lost the other two by sight as soon as they crept into the dark shrubbery, but he could hear their cautious movements nearby. Nothing else in the gorge seemed to move at all, not even the water, which flowed without a ripple over an invisible bed. There was not even any wind, for which Honath was grateful, although he had begun to develop an immunity to the motionless ground beneath them.

After a few moments, Honath heard a low whistle. Creeping sidewise toward the source of the sound, he nearly bumped into Alaskon, who was crouched beneath a thickly-spreading magnolia. An instant later, Mathilda's face peered out of the dim greenery.

"Look," Alaskon whispered. "What do you make of this?"

'This' was a hollow in the sandy soil, about four feet across and rimmed with a low parapet of earth-evidently the same earth that had been scooped out of its center. Occupying most of it were three grey, ellipsoidal objects, smooth and featureless.

"Eggs," Mathild said wonderingly.

"Obviously. But look at the size of them! Whatever laid them must be gigantic. I think we're trespassing in something's private valley."

Mathild drew in her breath. Honath thought fast, as much to prevent panic in himself as in the girl. A sharp-edged stone lying nearby provided the answer. He seized it and struck.

The outer surface of the egg was leathery rather than brittle; it tore raggedly. Deliberately, Honath bent and put his mouth to the oozing surface.

It was excellent. The flavor was decidedly stronger than that of birds' eggs, but he was far too hungry to be squeamish. After a moment's amazement, Alaskon and Mathild attacked the other two ovoids with a will. It was the first really satisfying meal they had had in Hell. When they finally moved away from the devastated nest, Honath felt better than he had since the day he was arrested.

As they moved on down the gorge, they began again to hear the roar of water, though the stream looked as placid as ever. Here, too, they saw the first sign of active life in the valley: a flight of giant dragonflies skimming over the water. The insects took fright as soon as Honath showed himself, but quickly came back, their nearly non-existent brains already convinced that there had always been men in the valley.

The roar got louder very rapidly. When the three rounded the long, gentle turn which had cut off their view from the exit, the source of the roar came into view. It was a sheet of falling water as tall as the depth of the gorge itself, which came arcing out from between two pillars of basalt and fell to a roiling, frothing pool.

"This is as far as we go!" Alaskon said, shouting to make himself heard over the tumult. "We'll never be able to get up these walls!"

Stunned, Honath looked from side to side. What Alaskon had said was all too obviously true. The gorge evidently had begun life as a layer of soft, partly soluble stone in the cliffs, tilted upright by some volcanic upheaval, and then worn completely away by the rushing stream. Both cliff faces were of the harder rock, and were sheer and as smooth as if they had been polished by hand. Here and there a network of tough vines had begun to climb them, but nowhere did such a network even come close to reaching the top.

Honath turned and looked once more at the great arc of water and spray. If there were only some way to prevent their being forced to retrace their steps —

Abruptly, over the riot of the falls, there was a piercing, hissing shriek. Echoes picked it up and sounded it again and again, all the way up the battlements of the cliffs. Honath sprang straight up in the air and came down trembling, facing away from the pool.

At first he could see nothing. Then, down at the open end of the turn, there was a huge flurry of motion.

A second later, a two-legged, blue-green reptile half as tall as the gorge itself came around the turn in a single bound and lunged violently into the far wall of the valley. It stopped as if momentarily stunned, and the great grinning head turned toward them a face of sinister and furious idiocy.

The shriek set the air to boiling again. Balancing itself with its heavy tail, the beast lowered its head and looked redly toward the falls.

The owner of the robbed nest had come home. They had met a demon of Hell at last.

Honath's mind at that instant went as white and blank as the under-bark of a poplar. He acted without thinking, without even knowing what he did. When thought began to creep back into his head again, the three of them were standing shivering in semidarkness, watching the blurred shadow of the demon lurching back and forth upon the screen of shining water.

It had been nothing but luck, not foreplanning, to find that there was a considerable space between the back of the falls proper and the blind wall of the canyon. It had been luck, too, which had forced Honath to skirt the pool in order to reach the falls at all, and thus had taken them all behind the silver curtain at the point where the weight of the falling water was too low to hammer them down for good. And it had been the blindest stroke of all that the demon had charged after them directly into the pool, where the deep, boiling water had slowed its thrashing hind legs enough to halt it before it went under the falls, as it had earlier blundered into the hard wall of the gorge.

Not an iota of all this had been in Honath's mind before he had discovered it to be true. At the moment that the huge reptile had screamed for the second time, he had simply grasped

Mathild's hand and broken for the falls, leaping from low tree to shrub to fern faster than he had ever leapt before. He did not stop to see how well Mathild was keeping up with him, or whether or not Alaskon was following. He only ran. He might have screamed, too; he could not remember.

They stood now, all three of them, wet through, behind the curtain until the shadow of the demon faded and vanished. Finally Honath felt a hand thumping his shoulder, and turned slowly.

Speech was impossible here, but Alaskon's pointing finger was eloquent enough. Along the back wall of the falls, where centuries of erosion had failed to wear away completely the original soft limestone, there was a sort of serrated chimney, open toward the gorge, which looked as though it could be climbed. At the top of the falls, the water shot out from between the basalt pillars in a smooth, almost solid-looking tube, arching at least six feet before beginning to break into the fan of spray and rainbows which poured down into the gorge. Once the chimney had been climbed, it should be possible to climb out from under the falls without passing through the water again.

And after that —?

Abruptly, Honath grinned. He felt weak all through with reaction, and the face of the demon would probably be grinning in his dreams for a long time to come. But at the same time he could not repress a surge of irrational confidence. He gestured upward jauntily, shook himself, and loped forward into the throat of the chimney.

Hardly more than an hour later they were all standing on a ledge overlooking the gorge, with the waterfall creaming over the brink next to them, only a few yards away. From here, it was evident that the gorge itself was only the bottom of a far greater cleft, a split in the pink-and-grey cliffs as sharp as though it had been riven in the rock by a bolt of sheet lightning. Beyond the basalt pillars from which the fall issued, however, the stream foamed over a long ladder of rock shelves which seemed to lead straight up into the sky.

"That way?" Mathild said.

"Yes, and as fast as possible," Alaskon said, shading his eyes. "It must be late. I don't think the light will last much longer."

"We'll have to go single file," Honath added. "And we'd better keep hold of each other's hands. One slip on those wet steps and-it's a long way down again."

Mathild shuddered and took Honath's hand convulsively. To his astonishment, the next instant she was tugging him toward the basalt pillars.

The irregular patch of deepening violet sky grew slowly as they climbed. They paused often, clinging to the jagged escarpments until their breath came back, and snatching icy water in cupped palms from the stream that fell down the ladder beside them. There was no way to tell how far up into the dusk the way had taken them, but Honath suspected that they were already somewhat above the level of their own vine-web world. The air smelled colder and sharper than it ever had above the jungle.

The final cut in the cliffs through which the stream fell was another chimney. It was steeper and more smooth-walled than the one which had taken them out of the gorge under the water-fall, but narrow enough to be climbed by bracing one's back against one side, and one's hands and feet against the other. The column of air inside the chimney was filled with spray, but in Hell that was too minor a discomfort to bother about.

At long last Honath heaved himself over the edge of the chimney onto flat rock, drenched and exhausted, but filled with an elation he could not suppress and did not want to. They were above the attic jungle; they had beaten Hell itself. He looked around to make sure that Mathild was safe, and then reached a hand down to Alaskon. The navigator's bad leg had been giving him trouble. Honath heaved mightily and Alaskon came heavily over the edge and lit sprawling on the high mesa.

The stars were out. For a while they simply sat and gasped for breath. Then they turned, one by one, to see where they were.

There was not a great deal to see. There was the mesa, domed with stars on all sides and a shining, finned spindle, like a gigantic minnow, pointing skyward in the center of the rocky plateau. And around the spindle, indistinct in the starlight....

...Around the shining minnow, tending it, were Giants.

This, then, was the end of the battle to do what was right, whatever the odds. All the show of courage against superstition, all the black battles against Hell itself, came down to this: *The Giants were real!*

They were unarguably real. Though they were twice as tall as men, stood straighter, had broader shoulders, were heavier across the seat and had no visible tails, their fellowship with men was clear. Even their voices, as they shouted to each other around their towering metal minnow, were the voices of men made into gods, voices as remote from those of men as the voices of men were remote from those of monkeys, yet just as clearly of the same family.

These were the Giants of the Book of Laws. They were not only real, but they had come back to Tellura as they had promised to do.

And they would know what to do with unbelievers, and with fugitives from Hell. It had all been for nothing-not only the physical struggle, but the fight to be allowed to think for oneself as well. The gods existed, literally, actually. This belief was the real hell from which Honath had been trying to fight free all his life-but now it was no longer just a belief. It was a fact, a fact that he was seeing with his own eyes.

The Giants had returned to judge their handiwork. And the first of the people they would meet would be three outcasts, three condemned and degraded criminals, three jail-breakers — the worst possible detritus of the attic world.

All this went searing through Honath's mind in less than a second, but nevertheless Alaskon's mind evidently had worked still faster. Always the most outspoken unbeliever of the entire little group of rebels, the one among them whose whole world was founded upon the existence of rational explanations for everything, his was the point of view most completely challenged by the sight before them now. With a deep, sharply indrawn breath, he turned abruptly and walked away from them.

Mathild uttered a cry of protest, which she choked off in the middle; but it was already too late. A round eye on the great silver minnow came alight, bathing them all in an oval patch of brilliance.

Honath darted after the navigator. Without looking back, Alaskon suddenly was running. For an instant longer Honath saw his figure, poised delicately against the black sky. Then he dropped silently out of sight, as suddenly and completely as if he had never been.

Alaskon had borne every hardship and every terror of the ascent from Hell with courage and even with cheerfulness but he had been unable to face being told that it had all been meaningless.

Sick at heart, Honath turned back, shielding his eyes from the miraculous light. There was a clear call in some unknown language from near the spindle.

Then there were footsteps, several pairs of them, coming closer.

It was time for the Second Judgment.

After a long moment, a big voice from the darkness said: "Don't be afraid. We mean you no harm. We're men, just as you are."

The language had the archaic flavor of the Book of Laws, but it was otherwise perfectly understandable. A second voice said: "What are you called?"

Honath's tongue seemed to be stuck to the roof of his mouth. While he was struggling with it, Mathild's voice came clearly from beside him:

"He is Honath the Pursemaker, and I am Mathild the Forager."

"You are a long distance from the place we left your people," the first Giant said. "Don't you still live in the vine-webs above the jungles?"

"Lord —"

"My name is Jarl Eleven. This man is Gerhardt Adler."

This seemed to stop Mathild completely. Honath could understand why. The very notion of addressing Giants by name was nearly paralyzing. But since they were already as good as cast down into Hell again, nothing could be lost by it.

"Jarl Eleven," he said, "the people still live among the vines. The floor of the jungle is forbidden. Only criminals are sent there. We are criminals."

"Oh?" Jarl Eleven said. "And you've come all the way from the surface to this mesa? Gerhardt, this is prodigious. You have no idea what the surface of this planet is like-it's a place where evolution has never managed to leave the tooth-and-nail stage. Dinosaurs from every period of the Mesozoic, primitive mammals all the way up the scale to the ancient cats the works. That's why the original seeding team put these people in the treetops instead."

"Honath, what was your crime?" Gerhardt Adler said.

Honath was almost relieved to have the questioning come so quickly to this point. Jarl Eleven's aside, with its many terms he could not understand, had been frightening in its very meaninglessness.

"There were five of us," Honath said in a low voice. "We said we-that we did not believe in the Giants."

There was a brief silence. Then, shockingly, both Jarl Eleven and Gerhardt Adler burst into enormous laughter.

Mathild cowered, her hands over her ears. Even Honath flinched and took a step backward. Instantly, the laughter stopped, and the Giant called Jarl Eleven stepped into the oval of light and sat down beside them. In the light, it could be seen that his face and hands were hairless, although there was hair on his crown; the rest of his body was covered by a kind of cloth. Seated, he was no taller than Honath, and did not seem quite so fearsome.

"I beg your pardon," he said. "It was unkind of us to laugh, but what you said was highly unexpected. Gerhardt, come over here and squat down, so that you don't look so much like a statue of some general. Tell me, Honath, in what way did you not believe in the Giants?"

Honath could hardly believe his ears. A Giant had begged his pardon! Was this still some joke even more cruel? But whatever the reason, Jarl Eleven had asked him a question.

"Each of the five of us differed," he said. "I held that you were not-not real except as symbols of some abstract truth. One of us, the wisest, believed that you did not exist in any sense at all. But we all agreed that you were not gods."

"And of course we aren't," Jarl Eleven said. "We're men. We come from the same stock as you. We're not your rulers, but your brothers. Do you understand what I say?"

"No," Honath admitted.

"Then let me tell you about it. There are men on many worlds, Honath. They differ from one another, because the worlds differ, and different kinds of men are needed to people each one. Gerhardt and I are the kind of men who live on a world called Earth, and many other worlds like it. We are two very minor members of a huge project called a 'seeding program', which has been going on for thousands of years now. It's the job of the seeding program to survey newly discovered worlds, and then to make men suitable to live on each new world."

"To make men? But only gods —"

"No, no. Be patient and listen," said Jarl Eleven. "We don't make men. We make them suitable. There's a great deal of difference between the two. We take the living germ plasm, the sperm and the egg, and we modify it. When the modified man emerges, we help him to settle down in his new world. That's what we did on Tellura-it happened long ago, before Gerhardt and I were even born. Now we've come back to see how you people are getting along, and to lend a hand if necessary."

He looked from Honath to Mathild, and back again. "Do you understand?" he said.

"I'm trying." Honath said. "But you should go down to the jungle-top, then. We're not like the others; they are the people you want to see."

"We shall, in the morning. We just landed here. But, just because you're not like the others, we're more interested in you now. Tell me, has any condemned man ever escaped from the jungle floor before you people?"

"No, never. That's not surprising. There are monsters down there."

Jarl Eleven looked sidewise at the other Giant. He seemed to be smiling. "When you see the films," he remarked, "you'll call that the understatement of the century. Honath, how did you three manage to escape, then?"

Haltingly at first, and then with more confidence as the memories came crowding vividly back, Honath told him. When he mentioned the feast at the demon's nest, Jarl Eleven again looked significantly at Adler, but he did not interrupt.

"And finally we got to the top of the chimney and came out on this flat space," Honath said. "Alaskon was still with us then, but when he saw you and the metal thing he threw himself back down the cleft. He was a criminal like us, but he should not have died. He was a brave man, and a wise one."

"Not wise enough to wait until all the evidence was in," Adler said enigmatically. "All in all, Jarl, I'd say 'prodigious' is the word for it. This is easily the most successful seeding job any team has ever done, at least in this limb of the galaxy. And what a stroke of luck, to be on the spot just as it came to term, and with a couple at that!"

"What does he mean?" Honath said.

"Just this, Honath. When the seeding team set your people up in business on Tellura, they didn't mean for you to live forever in the treetops. They knew that, sooner or later, you'd have to come down to the ground and learn to fight this planet on its own terms. Otherwise, you'd go stale and die out."

"Live on the ground all the time?" Mathild said in a faint voice.

"Yes, Mathild. The life in the treetops was to have been only an interim period, while you gathered knowledge you needed about Tellura and put it to use. But to be the real masters of the world, you will have to conquer the surface, too.

"The device your people worked out, that of sending criminals to the surface, was the best way of conquering the planet that they could have picked. It takes a strong will and courage to go against custom, and both those qualities are needed to lick Tellura. Your people exiled just such fighting spirits to the surface, year after year after year.

"Sooner or later, some of those exiles were going to discover how to live successfully on the ground and make it possible for the rest of your people to leave the trees. You and Honath have done just that."

"Observe please, Jarl," Adler said. "The crime in this first successful case was ideological. That was the crucial turn in the criminal policy of these people. A spirit of revolt is not quite enough, but couple it with brains and —*ecce homo!*"

Honath's head was swimming. "But what does all this mean?" he said. "Are we-not condemned to Hell any more?"

"No, you're still condemned, if you still want to call it that," Jarl Eleven said soberly. "You've learned how to live down there, and you've found out something even more valuable: how to stay alive while cutting down your enemies. Do you know that you killed three demons with your bare hands, you and Mathild and Alaskon?"

"Killed —"

"Certainly," Jarl Eleven said. "You ate three eggs. That is the classical way, and indeed the only way, to wipe out monsters like the dinosaurs. You can't kill the adults with anything short of an anti-tank gun, but they're helpless in embryo-and the adults haven't the sense to guard their nests."

Honath heard, but only distantly. Even his awareness of Mathild's warmth next to him did not seem to help much.

"Then we have to go back down there," he said dully. "And this time forever."

"Yes," Jarl Eleven said, his voice gentle. "But you wont be alone, Honath. Beginning tomorrow, you'll have all your people with you."

"*All* our people? But you're going to drive them out?"

"All of them. Oh, we won't prohibit the use of the vine-webs too, but from now on your race will have to fight it out on the surface as well. You and Mathild have proven that it can be done. It's high time the rest of you learned, too."

"Jarl, you think too little of these young people themselves," Adler said. "Tell them what is in store for them. They are frightened."

"Of course, of course. It's obvious. Honath, you and Mathild are the only living individuals of your race who know how to survive down there on the surface. And we're not going to tell your people how to do that. We aren't even going to drop them so much as a hint. That part of it is up to you."

Honath's jaw dropped.

"It's up to you," Jarl Eleven repeated firmly. "We'll return you to your tribe tomorrow, and we'll tell your people that you two know the rules for successful life on the ground-and that everyone else has to go down and live there too. We'll tell them nothing else but that. What do you think they'll do then?"

"I don't know," Honath said dazedly. "Anything could happen. They might even make us Spokesman and Spokeswoman-except that we're just common criminals."

"Uncommon pioneers, Honath. The man and the woman to lead the humanity of Tellura out of the attic, into the wide world." Jarl Eleven got to his feet, the great light playing over him. Looking up after him, Honath saw that there were at least a dozen other Giants standing just outside the oval of light, listening intently to every word.

"But there's a little time to be passed before we begin," Jarl Eleven said. "Perhaps you two would like to look over our ship."

Humbly, but with a soundless emotion much like music inside him, Honath took Mathild's hand. Together they walked away from the chimney to Hell, following the footsteps of the Giants.

To Pay the Piper

The man in the white jacket stopped at the door marked "Re-Education Project-Col. H. H. Mudgett, Commanding Officer" and waited while the scanner looked him over. He had been through that door a thousand times, but the scanner made as elaborate a job of it as if it had never seen him before.

It always did, for there was always in fact a chance that it *had* never seen him before, whatever the fallible human beings to whom it reported might think. It went over him from grey, crew-cut poll to reagent-proof shoes, checking his small wiry body and lean profile against its stored silhouettes, tasting and smelling him as dubiously as if he were an orange held in storage two days too long.

"Name?" it said at last.

"Carson, Samuel, 32-454-0698."

"Business?"

"Medical director, Re-Ed One."

While Carson waited, a distant, heavy concussion came rolling down upon him through the mile of solid granite above his head. At the same moment, the letters on the door-and everything else inside his cone of vision-blurred distressingly, and a stab of pure pain went lancing through his head. It was the supersonic component of the explosion, and it was harmless-except that it always both hurt and scared him.

The light on the door-scanner, which had been glowing yellow up to now, flicked back to red again and the machine began the whole routine all over; the sound-bomb had reset it. Carson patiently endured its inspection, gave his name, serial number and mission once more, and this time got the green. He went in, unfolding as he walked the flimsy square of cheap paper he had been carrying all along.

Mudgett looked up from his desk and said at once: "What now?"

The physician tossed the square of paper down under Mudgett's eyes. "Summary of the press reaction to Hamelin's speech last night," he said. "The total effect is going against us, Colonel. Unless we can change Hamelin's mind, this outcry to re-educate civilians ahead of soldiers is going to lose the war for us. The urge to live on the surface again has been mounting for ten years; now it's got a target to focus on. Us."

Mudgett chewed on a pencil while he read the summary; a blocky, bulky man, as short as Carson and with hair as grey and close-cropped. A year ago, Carson would have told him that nobody in Re-Ed could afford to put stray objects in his mouth even once, let alone as a habit; now Carson just waited. There wasn't a man-or a woman or a child-of America's surviving thirty-five million "sane" people who didn't have some such tic. Not now, not after twenty-five years of underground life.

"He knows it's impossible, doesn't he?" Mudgett demanded abruptly.

"Of course he doesn't," Carson said impatiently. "He doesn't know any more about the real nature of the project than the people do. He thinks the 'educating' we do is in some sort of survival technique-That's what the papers think, too, as you can plainly see by the way they loaded that editorial."

"Um. If we'd taken direct control of the papers in the first place —"

Carson said nothing. Military control of every facet of civilian life was a fact, and Mudgett knew it. He also knew that an appearance of freedom to think is a necessity for the human mind-and that the appearance could not be maintained without a few shreds of the actuality.

"Suppose we do this," Mudgett said at last. "Hamelin's position in the State Department makes it impossible for us to muzzle him. But it ought to be possible to explain to him that no unprotected human being can live on the surface, no matter how many Merit Badges he has for woodcraft and first aid. Maybe we could even take him on a little trip topside; I'll wager he's never seen it."

"And what if he dies up there?" Carson said stonily. "We lose three-fifths of every topside party as it is-and Hamelin's an inexperienced —"

"Might be the best thing, mightn't it?"

"*No*," Carson said. "It would look like we'd planned it that way. The papers would have the populace boiling by the next morning."

Mudgett groaned and nibbled another double row of indentations around the barrel of the pencil. "There must be something," he said.

"There is."

"Well?"

"Bring the man here and show him just what we *are* doing. Re-educate *him*, if necessary. Once we told the newspapers that he'd taken the course ... well, who knows, they just might resent it. Abusing his clearance privileges and so on."

"We'd be violating our basic policy," Mudgett said slowly. "'Give the Earth back to the men who fight for it.' Still, the idea has some merits...."

"Hamelin is out in the antechamber right now," Carson said. "Shall I bring him in?"

The radioactivity never did rise much beyond a mildly hazardous level, and that was only transient, during the second week of the war-the week called the Death of Cities. The small shards of sanity retained by the high commands on both sides dictated avoiding weapons with a built-in backfire: no cobalt bombs were dropped, no territories permanently poisoned. Generals still remembered that unoccupied territory, no matter how devastated, is still unconquered territory.

But no such considerations stood in the way of biological warfare. It was controllable: you never released against the enemy any disease you didn't yourself know how to control. There would be some slips, of course, but the margin for error —

There were some slips. But for the most part, biological warfare worked fine. The great fevers washed like tides around and around the globe, one after another. In such cities as had escaped the bombings, the rumble of truck convoys carrying the puffed heaped corpses to the mass graves became the only sound except for sporadic small-arms fire; and then that too ceased, and the trucks stood rusting in rows.

Nor were human beings the sole victims. Cattle fevers were sent out. Wheat rusts, rice molds, corn blights, hog choleras, poultry enteritises fountained into the indifferent air from the hidden laboratories, or were loosed far aloft, in the jet-stream, by rocketing fleets. Gelatin capsules pullulating with gill-rots fell like hail into the great fishing grounds of Newfoundland, Oregon, Japan, Sweden, Portugal. Hundreds of species of animals were drafted as secondary hosts for human diseases, were injected and released to carry the blessings of the laboratories to their mates and litters. It was discovered that minute amounts of the tetracycline series of antibiotics, which had long been used as feed supplements to bring farm animals to full market weight early, could also be used to raise the most whopping Anopheles and Aëdes mosquitoes anybody ever saw, capable of flying long distances against the wind and of carrying a peculiarly interesting new strains of the malarial parasite and the yellow fever virus....

By the time it had ended, everyone who remained alive was a mile under ground.

For good.

"I still fail to understand why," Hamelin said, "if, as you claim, you have methods of re-educating soldiers for surface life, you can't do so for civilians as well. Or instead."

The under-secretary, a tall, spare man, bald on top, and with a heavily creased forehead, spoke with the odd neutral accent-untinged by regionalism-of the trained diplomat, despite the fact that there had been no such thing as a foreign service for nearly half a century.

"We're going to try to explain that to you," Carson said. "But we thought that, first of all, we'd try to explain once more why we think it would be bad policy-as well as physically out of the question.

"Sure, everybody wants to go topside as soon as it's possible. Even people who are reconciled to these endless caverns and corridors hope for something better for their children —a glimpse of sunlight, a little rain, the fall of a leaf. That's more important now to all of us than the war, which we don't believe in any longer. That doesn't even make any military sense, since we haven't the numerical strength to occupy the enemy's territory any more, and they haven't the strength to occupy ours. We understand all that. But we also know that the enemy is intent on prosecuting the war to the end. Extermination is what they say they want, on their propaganda broadcasts, and your own Department reports that they seem to mean what they say. So we can't give up fighting them; that would be simple suicide. Are you still with me?"

"Yes, but I don't see —"

"Give me a moment more. If we have to continue to fight, we know this much: that the first of the two sides to get men on the surface again-so as to be able to *attack* important targets, not just keep them isolated in seas of plagues-will be the side that will bring this war to an end. They know that, too. We have good reason to believe that they have a re-education project, and that it's about as far advanced as ours is."

"Look at it this way," Col. Mudgett burst in unexpectedly. "What we have now is a stalemate. A saboteur occasionally locates one of the underground cities and lets the pestilences into it. Sometimes on our side, sometimes on theirs. But that only happens sporadically, and it's just more of this mutual extermination business-to which we're committed, willy-nilly, for as long as they are. If we can get troops onto the surface first, we'll be able to scout out their important installations in short order, and issue them a surrender ultimatum with teeth in it. They'll take it. The only other course is the sort of slow, mutual suicide we've got now."

Hamelin put the tips of his fingers together. "You gentlemen lecture me about policy as if I had never heard the word before. I'm familiar with your arguments for sending soldiers first. You assume that you're familiar with all of mine for starting with civilians, but you're wrong, because some of them haven't been brought up at all outside the Department. I'm going to tell you some of them, and I think they'll merit your close attention."

Carson shrugged. "I'd like nothing better than to be convinced, Mr. Secretary. Go ahead."

"You of all people should know, Dr. Carson, how close our underground society is to a psychotic break. To take a single instance, the number of juvenile gangs roaming these corridors of ours has increased 400% since the rumors about the Re-Education Project began to spread. Or another: the number of individual crimes without motive-crimes committed, just to distract the committer from the grinding monotony of the life we all lead-has now passed the total of all other crimes put together.

"And as for actual insanity-of our thirty-five million people still unhospitalized, there are four million cases *of which we know,* each one of which should be committed right now for early paranoid schizophrenia-except that were we to commit them, our essential industries would suffer a manpower loss more devastating than anything the enemy has inflicted upon us. Every one of those four million persons is a major hazard to his neighbors and to his job, but how can we do without them? And what can we do about the unrecognized, sub-clinical cases, which probably total twice as many? How long can we continue operating without a collapse under such conditions?"

Carson mopped his brow. "I didn't suspect that it had gone that far."

"It has gone that far," Hamelin said icily, "and it is accelerating. Your own project has helped to accelerate it. Col. Mudgett here mentioned the opening of isolated cities to the pestilences. Shall I tell you how Louisville fell?"

"A spy again, I suppose," Mudgett said.

"No, Colonel. Not a spy. A band of-of vigilantes, of mutineers. I'm familiar with your slogan, 'The Earth to those who fight for it.' Do you know the counter-slogan that's circulating among the people?"

They waited. Hamelin smiled and said: "'Let's die on the surface.'

"They overwhelmed the military detachment there, put the city administration to death, and blew open the shaft to the surface. About a thousand people actually made it to the top. Within twenty-four hours the city was dead-as the ringleaders had been warned would be the outcome. The warning didn't deter them. Nor did it protect the prudent citizens who had no part in the affair."

Hamelin leaned forward suddenly. "People won't wait to be told when it's their turn to be re-educated. They'll be tired of waiting, tired to the point of insanity of living at the bottom of a hole. They'll just go.

"And that, gentlemen, will leave the world to the enemy ... or, more likely, the rats. They alone are immune to everything by now."

There was a long silence. At last Carson said mildly: "Why aren't *we* immune to everything by now?"

"Eh? Why-the new generations. They've never been exposed."

"We still have a reservoir of older people who lived through the war: people who had one or several of the new diseases that swept the world, some as many as five, and yet recovered. They still have their immunities; we know; we've tested them. We know from sampling that no new disease has been introduced by either side in over ten years now. Against all the known ones, we have immunization techniques, anti-sera, antibiotics, and so on. I suppose you get your shots every six months like all the rest of us; we should all be very hard to infect now, and such infections as do take should run mild courses." Carson held the under-secretary's eyes grimly. "Now, answer me this question: why is it that, despite all these protections, *every single person* in an opened city dies?"

"I don't know," Hamelin said, staring at each of them in turn. "By your showing, some of them should recover."

"They should," Carson said. "But nobody does. Why? Because the very nature of disease has changed since we all went underground. There are now abroad in the world a number of mutated bacterial strains which can bypass the immunity mechanisms of the human body altogether. What this means in simple terms is that, should such a germ get into your body, your body wouldn't recognize it as an invader. It would manufacture no antibodies against the germ. Consequently, the germ could multiply without any check, and-you would die. So would we all."

"I see," Hamelin said. He seemed to have recovered his composure extraordinarily rapidly. "I am no scientist, gentlemen, but what you tell me makes our position sound perfectly hopeless. Yet obviously you have some answer."

Carson nodded. "We do. But it's important for you to understand the situation, otherwise the answer will mean nothing to you. So: is it perfectly clear to you now, from what we've said so far, that no amount of re-educating a man's brain, be he soldier *or* civilian, will allow him to survive on the surface?"

"Quite clear," Hamelin said, apparently ungrudgingly. Carson's hopes rose by a fraction of a millimeter. "But if you don't re-educate his brain, what can you re-educate? His reflexes, perhaps?"

"No," Carson said. "His lymph nodes, and his spleen."

A scornful grin began to appear on Hamelin's thin lips. "You need better public relations counsel than you've been getting," he said. "If what you say is true-as of course I assume it is-then the term 're-educate' is not only inappropriate, it's downright misleading. If you had chosen a less suggestive and more accurate label in the beginning, I wouldn't have been able to cause you half the trouble I have."

"I agree that we were badly advised there," Carson said. "But not entirely for those reasons. Of course the name is misleading; that's both a characteristic and a function of the names of top secret projects. But in this instance, the name 'Re-Education', bad as it now appears, subjected the men who chose it to a fatal temptation. You see, though it is misleading, it is also entirely accurate."

"Word-games," Hamelin said.

"Not at all," Mudgett interposed. "We were going to spare you the theoretical reasoning behind our project, Mr. Secretary, but now you'll just have to sit still for it. The fact is that the body's ability to distinguish between its own cells and those of some foreign tissue —a skin graft, say, or a bacterial invasion of the blood-isn't an inherited ability. It's a learned reaction. Furthermore, if you'll think about it a moment, you'll see that it has to be. Body cells die, too, and have to be disposed of; what would happen if removing those dead cells provoked an antibody reaction, as the destruction of foreign cells does? We'd die of anaphylactic shock while we were still infants.

"For that reason, the body has to learn how to scavenge selectively. In human beings, that lesson isn't learned completely until about a month after birth. During the intervening time, the newborn infant is protected by antibodies that it gets from the colestrum, the 'first milk' it gets from the breast during the three or four days immediately after birth. It can't generate its own; it isn't allowed to, so to speak, until it's learned the trick of cleaning up body residues *without* triggering the antibody mechanisms. Any dead cells marked 'personal' have to be dealt with some other way."

"That seems clear enough," Hamelin said. "But I don't see its relevance."

"Well, we're in a position now where that differentiation between the self and everything outside the body doesn't do us any good any more. These mutated bacteria have been 'selfed' by the mutation. In other words, some of their protein molecules, probably desoxyribonucleic acid molecules, carry configurations or 'recognition-units' identical with those of our body cells, so that the body can't tell one from another."

"But what has all this to do with re-education?"

"Just this," Carson said. "What we do here is to impose upon the cells of the body-all of them —a new set of recognition-units for the guidance of the lymph nodes and the spleen, which are the organs that produce antibodies. The new units are highly complex, and the chances of their being duplicated by bacterial evolution, even under forced draught, are too small to worry about. That's what Re-Education is. In a few moments, if you like, we'll show you just how it's done."

Hamelin ground out his fifth cigarette in Mudgett's ashtray and placed the tips of his fingers together thoughtfully. Carson wondered just how much of the concept of recognition-marking the under-secretary had absorbed. It had to be admitted that he was astonishingly quick to take hold of abstract ideas, but the self-marker theory of immunity was-like everything else in immunology-almost impossible to explain to laymen, no matter how intelligent.

"This process," Hamelin said hesitantly. "It takes a long time?"

"About six hours per subject, and we can handle only one man at a time. That means that we can count on putting no more than seven thousand troops into the field by the turn of the century. Every one will have to be a highly trained specialist, if we're to bring the war to a quick conclusion."

"Which means no civilians," Hamelin said. "I see. I'm not entirely convinced, but-by all means let's see how it's done."

Once inside, the under-secretary tried his best to look everywhere at once. The room cut into the rock was roughly two hundred feet high. Most of it was occupied by the bulk of the Re-Education Monitor, a mechanism as tall as a fifteen-storey building, and about a city block square. Guards watched it on all sides, and the face of the machine swarmed with technicians.

"Incredible," Hamelin murmured. "That enormous object can process only one man at a time?"

"That's right," Mudgett said. "Luckily it doesn't have to treat all the body cells directly. It works through the blood, re-selfing the cells by means of small changes in the serum chemistry."

"What kind of changes?"

"Well," Carson said, choosing each word carefully, "that's more or less a graveyard secret, Mr. Secretary. We can tell you this much: the machine uses a vast array of crystalline, complex sugars which *behave* rather like the blood group-and-type proteins. They're fed into the serum in minute amounts, under feedback control of second-by-second analysis of the blood. The computations involved in deciding upon the amount and the precise nature of each introduced chemical are highly complex. Hence the size of the machine. It is, in its major effect, an artificial kidney."

"I've seen artificial kidneys in the hospitals," Hamelin said, frowning. "They're rather compact affairs."

"Because all they do is remove waste products from the patient's blood, and restore the fluid and electrolyte balance. Those are very minor renal functions in the higher mammals. The organ's main duty is chemical control of immunity. If Burnet and Fenner had known that back in 1949, when the selfing theory was being formulated, we'd have had Re-Education long before now."

"Most of the machine's size is due to the computation section," Mudgett emphasized. "In the body, the brain-stem does those computations, as part of maintaining homeostasis. But we can't reach the brain-stem from outside; it's not under conscious control. Once the body is re-selfed, it will re-train the thalamus where we can't." Suddenly, two swinging doors at the base of the machine were pushed apart and a mobile operating table came through, guided by two attendants. There was a form on it, covered to the chin with a sheet. The face above the sheet was immobile and almost as white.

Hamelin watched the table go out of the huge cavern with visibly mixed emotions. He said: "This process-it's painful?"

"No, not exactly," Carson said. The motive behind the question interested him hugely, but he didn't dare show it. "But any fooling around with the immunity mechanisms can give rise to symptoms-fever, general malaise, and so on. We try to protect our subjects by giving them a light shock anesthesia first."

"Shock?" Hamelin repeated. "You mean electroshock? I don't see how —"

"Call it stress anesthesia instead. We give the man a steroid drug that counterfeits the anesthesia the body itself produces in moments of great stress-on the battlefield, say, or just after a serious injury. It's fast, and free of after-effects. There's no secret about that, by the way; the drug involved is 21-hydroxypregnane-3,20 dione sodium succinate, and it dates all the way back to 1955."

"Oh," the under-secretary said. The ringing sound of the chemical name had had, as Carson had hoped, a ritually soothing effect.

"Gentlemen," Hamelin said hesitantly. "Gentlemen, I have a —a rather unusual request. And, I am afraid, a rather selfish one." A brief, nervous laugh. "Selfish in both senses, if you will pardon me the pun. You need feel no hesitation in refusing me, but...."

Abruptly he appeared to find it impossible to go on. Carson mentally crossed his fingers and plunged in.

"You would like to undergo the process yourself?" he said.

"Well, yes. Yes, that's exactly it. Does that seem inconsistent? I should know, should I not, what it is that I'm advocating for my following? Know it intimately, from personal experience, not just theory? Of course I realize that it would conflict with your policy, but I assure you I wouldn't turn it to any political advantage-none whatsoever. And perhaps it wouldn't be too great a lapse of policy to process just one civilian among your seven thousand soldiers."

Subverted, by God! Carson looked at Mudgett with a firmly straight face. It wouldn't do to accept too quickly.

But Hamelin was rushing on, almost chattering now. "I can understand your hesitation. You must feel that I'm trying to gain some advantage, or even to get to the surface ahead of my fellow-men. If it will set your minds at rest, I would be glad to enlist in your advance army. Before five years are up, I could surely learn some technical skill which would make me useful to the expedition. If you would prepare papers to that effect, I'd be happy to sign them."

"That's hardly necessary," Mudgett said. "After you're Re-Educated, we can simply announce the fact, and say that you've agreed to join the advance party when the time comes."

"Ah," Hamelin said. "I see the difficulty. No, that would make my position quite impossible. If there is no other way —"

"Excuse us a moment," Carson said. Hamelin bowed, and the doctor pulled Mudgett off out of ear-shot.

"Don't overplay it," he murmured. "You're tipping our hand with that talk about a press release, Colonel. He's offering us a bribe-but he's plenty smart enough to see that the price you're suggesting is that of his whole political career. He won't pay that much."

"What then?" Mudgett whispered hoarsely.

"Get somebody to prepare the kind of informal contract he suggested. Offer to put it under security seal so we won't be able to show it to the press at all. He'll know well enough that such a seal can be broken if our policy ever comes before a presidential review-and that will restrain him from forcing such a review. Let's not demand too much. Once he's been re-educated, he'll have to live the rest of the five years with the knowledge that he *can* live topside any time he wants to try it-and he hasn't had the discipline our men have had. It's my bet that he'll goof off before the five years are up-and good riddance."

They went back to Hamelin, who was watching the machine and humming in a painfully abstracted manner.

"I've convinced the Colonel," Carson said, "that your services in the army might well be very valuable when the time comes, Mr. Secretary. If you'll sign up, we'll put the papers under security seal for your own protection, and then I think we can fit you into our treatment program today."

"I'm grateful to you, Dr. Carson," Hamelin said. "Very grateful, indeed."

Five minutes after his injection, Hamelin was as peaceful as a flounder and was rolled through the swinging doors. An hour's discussion of the probable outcome, carried on in the privacy of Mudgett's office, bore very little additional fruit, however.

"It's our only course," Carson said. "It's what we hoped to gain from his visit, duly modified by circumstances. It all comes down to this: Hamelin's compromised himself, and he knows it."

"But," Mudgett said, "suppose he was right? What about all that talk of his about mass insanity?"

"I'm sure it's true," Carson said, his voice trembling slightly despite his best efforts at control. "It's going to be rougher than ever down here for the next five years, Colonel. Our only consolation is that the enemy must have exactly the same problem; and if we can beat them to the surface —"

"*Hsst!*" Mudgett said. Carson had already broken off his sentence. He wondered why the scanner gave a man such a hard time outside that door, and then admitted him without any warning to the people on the other side. Couldn't the damned thing be trained to knock?

The newcomer was a page from the haemotology section. "Here's the preliminary rundown on your 'Student X', Dr. Carson," he said.

The page saluted Mudgett and went out. Carson began to read. After a moment, he also began to sweat.

"Colonel, look at this. I was wrong after all. Disastrously wrong. I haven't seen a blood-type distribution pattern like Hamelin's since I was a medical student, and even back then it was only a demonstration, not a real live patient. Look at it from the genetic point of view-the migration factors."

He passed the protocol across the desk. Mudgett was not by background a scientist, but he was an enormously able administrator, of the breed that makes it its business to know the technicalities on which any project ultimately rests. He was not much more than half-way through the tally before his eyebrows were gaining altitude like shock-waves.

"Carson, we can't let that man into the machine! He's —"

"He's already in it, Colonel, you know that. And if we interrupt the process before it runs to term, we'll kill him."

"Let's kill him, then," Mudgett said harshly. "Say he died while being processed. Do the country a favor."

"That would produce a hell of a stink. Besides, we have no proof."

Mudgett flourished the protocol excitedly.

"That's not proof to anyone but a haemotologist."

"But Carson, the man's a saboteur!" Mudgett shouted. "Nobody but an Asiatic could have a typing pattern like this! And he's no melting-pot product, either-he's a classical mixture, very probably a Georgian. And every move he's made since we first heard of him has been aimed directly at us-aimed directly at tricking us into getting him into the machine!"

"I think so too," Carson said grimly. "I just hope the enemy hasn't many more agents as brilliant."

"One's enough," Mudgett said. "He's sure to be loaded to the last cc of his blood with catalyst poisons. Once the machine starts processing his serum, we're done for-it'll take us years to re-program the computer, if it can be done at all. It's *got* to be stopped!"

"Stopped?" Carson said, astonished. "But it's already stopped. That's not what worries me. The machine stopped it fifty minutes ago."

"It can't have! How could it? It has no relevant data!"

"Sure it has." Carson leaned forward, took the cruelly chewed pencil away from Mudgett, and made a neat check beside one of the entries on the protocol. Mudgett stared at the checked item.

"Platelets Rh VI?" he mumbled. "But what's that got to do with.... Oh. Oh, I see. That platelet type doesn't exist at all in our population now, does it? Never seen it before myself, at least."

"No," Carson said, grinning wolfishly. "It never was common in the West, and the pogrom of 1981 wiped it out. That's something the enemy couldn't know. But the machine knows it. As soon as it gives him the standard anti-IV desensitization shot, his platelets will begin to dissolve-and he'll be rejected for incipient thrombocytopenia." He laughed. "For his own protection! But —"

"But he's getting nitrous oxide in the machine, and he'll be held six hours under anesthesia anyhow-also for his own protection," Mudgett broke in. He was grinning back at Carson like an idiot. "When he comes out from under, he'll assume that he's been re-educated, and he'll beat it back to the enemy to report that he's poisoned our machine, so that they can be sure they'll beat us to the surface. And he'll go the fastest way: *overland*."

"He will," Carson agreed. "Of course he'll go overland, and of course he'll die. But where does that leave us? We won't be able to conceal that he was treated here, if there's any sort of an inquiry at all. And his death will make everything we do here look like a fraud. Instead of paying our Pied Piper-and great jumping Jehosophat, look at his name! They were rubbing our noses in it all the time! Nevertheless, we didn't pay the piper; we killed him. And 'platelets Rh VI' won't be an adequate excuse for the press, or for Hamelin's following."

"It doesn't worry me," Mudgett rumbled. "Who'll know? He won't die in our labs. He'll leave here hale and hearty. He won't die until he makes a break for the surface. After that we can compose a fine obituary for the press. Heroic government official, on the highest policy level-couldn't wait to lead his followers to the surface-died of being too much in a hurry-Re-Ed Project sorrowfully reminds everyone that no technique is fool-proof —"

Mudgett paused long enough to light a cigarette, which was a most singular action for a man who never smoked. "As a matter of fact, Carson," he said, "it's a natural."

Carson considered it. It seemed to hold up. And 'Hamelin' would have a death certificate as complex as he deserved-not officially, of course, but in the minds of everyone who knew the facts. His death, when it came, would be due directly to the thrombocytopenia which had caused the Re-Ed machine to reject him-and thrombocytopenia is a disease of infants. *Unless ye become as little children....*

That was a fitting reason for rejection from the new kingdom of Earth: anemia of the newborn.

His pent breath went out of him in a long sigh. He hadn't been aware that he'd been holding it. "It's true," he said softly. "That's the time to pay the piper."

"When?" Mudgett said.

"When?" Carson said, surprised. "Why, *before* he takes the children away."

One-Shot

On the day that the Polish freighter *Ludmilla* laid an egg in New York harbor, Abner Longmans ("One-Shot") Braun was in the city going about his normal business, which was making another million dollars. As we found out later, almost nothing else was normal about that particular week end for Braun. For one thing, he had brought his family with him —a complete departure from routine-reflecting the unprecedentedly legitimate nature of the deals he was trying to make. From every point of view it was a bad week end for the CIA to mix into his affairs, but nobody had explained that to the master of the *Ludmilla*.

I had better add here that we knew nothing about this until afterward; from the point of view of the storyteller, an organization like Civilian Intelligence Associates gets to all its facts backwards, entering the tale at the pay-off, working back to the hook, and winding up with a sheaf of background facts to feed into the computer for Next Time. It's rough on the various people who've tried to fictionalize what we do-particularly for the lazy examples of the breed, who come to us expecting that their plotting has already been done for them-but it's inherent in the way we operate, and there it is.

Certainly nobody at CIA so much as thought of Braun when the news first came through. Harry Anderton, the Harbor Defense chief, called us at 0830 Friday to take on the job of identifying the egg; this was when our records show us officially entering the affair, but, of course, Anderton had been keeping the wires to Washington steaming for an hour before that, getting authorization to spend some of his money on us (our clearance status was then and is now C&R —clean and routine).

I was in the central office when the call came through, and had some difficulty in making out precisely what Anderton wanted of us. "Slow down, Colonel Anderton, please," I begged him. "Two or three seconds won't make that much difference. How did you find out about this egg in the first place?"

"The automatic compartment bulkheads on the *Ludmilla* were defective," he said. "It seems that this egg was buried among a lot of other crates in the dump-cell of the hold —"

"What's a dump cell?"

"It's a sea lock for getting rid of dangerous cargo. The bottom of it opens right to Davy Jones. Standard fitting for ships carrying explosives, radioactives, anything that might act up unexpectedly."

"All right," I said. "Go ahead."

"Well, there was a timer on the dump-cell floor, set to drop the egg when the ship came up the river. That worked fine, but the automatic bulkheads that are supposed to keep the rest of the ship from being flooded while the cell's open, didn't. At least they didn't do a thorough job. The *Ludmilla* began to list and the captain yelled for help. When the Harbor Patrol found the dump-cell open, they called us in."

"I see." I thought about it a moment. "In other words, you don't know whether the *Ludmilla* really laid an egg or not."

"That's what I keep trying to explain to you, Dr. Harris. We don't know what she dropped and we haven't any way of finding out. It could be a bomb-it could be anything. We're sweating everybody on board the ship now, but it's my guess that none of them know anything; the whole procedure was designed to be automatic."

"All right, we'll take it," I said. "You've got divers down?"

"Sure, but —"

"We'll worry about the buts from here on. Get us a direct line from your barge to the big board here so we can direct the work. Better get on over here yourself."

"Right." He sounded relieved. Official people have a lot of confidence in CIA; too much, in my estimation. Some day the job will come along that we can't handle, and then Washington will be kicking itself-or, more likely, some scapegoat-for having failed to develop a comparable government department.

Not that there was much prospect of Washington's doing that. Official thinking had been running in the other direction for years. The precedent was the Associated Universities organization which ran Brookhaven; CIA had been started the same way, by a loose corporation of universities and industries all of which had wanted to own an ULTIMAC and no one of which had had the money to buy one for itself. The Eisenhower administration, with its emphasis on private enterprise and concomitant reluctance to sink federal funds into projects of such size, had turned the two examples into a nice fat trend, which ULTIMAC herself said wasn't going to be reversed within the practicable lifetime of CIA.

I buzzed for two staffers, and in five minutes got Clark Cheyney and Joan Hadamard, CIA's business manager and social science division chief respectively. The titles were almost solely for the benefit of the T/O —that is, Clark and Joan do serve in those capacities, but said service takes about two per cent of their capacities and their time. I shot them a couple of sentences of explanation, trusting them to pick up whatever else they needed from the tape, and checked the line to the divers' barge.

It was already open; Anderton had gone to work quickly and with decision once he was sure we were taking on the major question. The television screen lit, but nothing showed on it but murky light, striped with streamers of darkness slowly rising and falling. The audio went *cloonck ... oing, oing ... bonk ... oing ...* Underwater noises, shapeless and characterless.

"Hello, out there in the harbor. This is CIA, Harris calling. Come in, please."

"Monig here," the audio said. *Boink ... oing, oing ...*

"Got anything yet?"

"Not a thing, Dr. Harris," Monig said. "You can't see three inches in front of your face down here-it's too silty. We've bumped into a couple of crates, but so far, no egg."

"Keep trying."

Cheyney, looking even more like a bulldog than usual, was setting his stopwatch by one of the eight clocks on ULTIMAC's face. "Want me to take the divers?" he said.

"No, Clark, not yet. I'd rather have Joan do it for the moment." I passed the mike to her. "You'd better run a probability series first."

"Check." He began feeding tape into the integrator's mouth. "What's your angle, Peter?"

"The ship. I want to see how heavily shielded that dump-cell is."

"It isn't shielded at all," Anderton's voice said behind me. I hadn't heard him come in. "But that doesn't prove anything. The egg might have carried sufficient shielding in itself. Or maybe the Commies didn't care whether the crew was exposed or not. Or maybe there isn't any egg."

"All that's possible," I admitted. "But I want to see it, anyhow."

"Have you taken blood tests?" Joan asked Anderton.

"Yes."

"Get the reports through to me, then. I want white-cell counts, differentials, platelet counts, hematocrit and sed rates on every man."

Anderton picked up the phone and I took a firm hold on the doorknob.

"Hey," Anderton said, putting the phone down again. "Are you going to duck out just like that? Remember, Dr. Harris, we've got to evacuate the city first of all! No matter whether it's a real egg or not-we can't take the chance on it's *not* being an egg!"

"Don't move a man until you get a go-ahead from CIA," I said. "For all we know now, evacuating the city may be just what the enemy wants us to do-so they can grab it unharmed. Or they may want to start a panic for some other reason, any one of fifty possible reasons."

"You can't take such a gamble," he said grimly. "There are eight and a half million lives riding on it. I can't let you do it."

"You passed your authority to us when you hired us," I pointed out. "If you want to evacuate without our O.K., you'll have to fire us first. It'll take another hour to get that cleared from Washington-so you might as well give us the hour."

He stared at me for a moment, his lips thinned. Then he picked up the phone again to order Joan's blood count, and I got out the door, fast.

A reasonable man would have said that I found nothing useful on the *Ludmilla*, except negative information. But the fact is that anything I found would have been a surprise to me; I went down looking for surprises. I found nothing but a faint trail to Abner Longmans Braun, most of which was fifteen years cold.

There'd been a time when I'd known Braun, briefly and to no profit to either of us. As an undergraduate majoring in social sciences, I'd taken on a term paper on the old International Longshoreman's Association, a racket-ridden union now formally extinct-although anyone who knew the signs could still pick up some traces on the docks. In those days, Braun had been the business manager of an insurance firm, the sole visible function of which had been to write policies for the ILA and its individual dock-wallopers. For some reason, he had been amused by the brash youngster who'd barged in on him and demanded the lowdown, and had shown me considerable lengths of ropes not normally in view of the public-nothing incriminating, but enough to give me a better insight into how the union operated than I had had any right to expect-or even suspect.

Hence I was surprised to hear somebody on the docks remark that Braun was in the city over the week end. It would never have occurred to me that he still interested himself in the waterfront, for he'd gone respectable with a vengeance. He was still a professional gambler, and according to what he had told the Congressional Investigating Committee last year, took in thirty to fifty thousand dollars a year at it, but his gambles were no longer concentrated on horses, the numbers, or shady insurance deals. Nowadays what he did was called investment-mostly in real estate; realtors knew him well as the man who had *almost* bought the Empire State Building. (The *almost* in the equation stands for the moment when the shoestring broke.)

Joan had been following his career, too, not because she had ever met him, but because for her he was a type study in the evolution of what she called "the extra-legal ego." "With personalities like that, respectability is a disease," she told me. "There's always an almost-open conflict between the desire to be powerful and the desire to be accepted; your ordinary criminal is a moral imbecile, but people like Braun are damned with a conscience, and sooner or later they crack trying to appease it."

"I'd sooner try to crack a Timkin bearing," I said. "Braun's ten-point steel all the way through."

"Don't you believe it. The symptoms are showing all over him. Now he's backing Broadway plays, sponsoring beginning actresses, joining playwrights' groups-he's the only member of Buskin and Brush who's never written a play, acted in one, or so much as pulled the rope to raise the curtain."

"That's investment," I said. "That's his business."

"Peter, you're only looking at the surface. His real investments almost never fail. But the plays he backs *always* do. They have to; he's sinking money in them to appease his conscience, and if they were to succeed it would double his guilt instead of salving it. It's the same way with the young actresses. He's not sexually interested in them-his type never is, because living a rigidly orthodox family life is part of the effort towards respectability. He's backing them to 'pay his debt to society' —in other words, they're talismans to keep him out of jail."

"It doesn't seem like a very satisfactory substitute."

"Of course it isn't," Joan had said. "The next thing he'll do is go in for direct public service-giving money to hospitals or something like that. You watch."

She had been right; within the year, Braun had announced the founding of an association for clearing the Detroit slum area where he had been born-the plainest kind of symbolic suicide: *Let's not have any more Abner Longmans Brauns born down here.* It depressed me to see it happen, for next on Joan's agenda for Braun was an entry into politics as a fighting liberal —a New

Dealer twenty years too late. Since I'm mildly liberal myself when I'm off duty, I hated to think what Braun's career might tell me about my own motives, if I'd let it.

All of which had nothing to do with why I was prowling around the *Ludmilla* —or did it? I kept remembering Anderton's challenge: "You can't take such a gamble. There are eight and a half million lives riding on it —" That put it up into Braun's normal operating area, all right. The connection was still hazy, but on the grounds that any link might be useful, I phoned him.

He remembered me instantly; like most uneducated, power-driven men, he had a memory as good as any machine's.

"You never did send me that paper you was going to write," he said. His voice seemed absolutely unchanged, although he was in his seventies now. "You promised you would."

"Kids don't keep their promises as well as they should," I said. "But I've still got copies and I'll see to it that you get one, this time. Right now I need another favor-something right up your alley."

"CIA business?"

"Yes. I didn't know you knew I was with CIA."

Braun chuckled. "I still know a thing or two," he said. "What's the angle?"

"That I can't tell you over the phone. But it's the biggest gamble there ever was, and I think we need an expert. Can you come down to CIA's central headquarters right away?"

"Yeah, if it's that big. If it ain't, I got lots of business here, Andy. And I ain't going to be in town long. You're sure it's top stuff?"

"My word on it."

He was silent a moment. Then he said, "Andy, send me your paper."

"The paper? Sure, but —" Then I got it. I'd given him my word. "You'll get it," I said. "Thanks, Mr. Braun."

I called headquarters and sent a messenger to my apartment to look for one of those long-dusty blue folders with the legal-length sheets inside them, with orders to scorch it over to Braun without stopping to breathe more than once. Then I went back myself.

The atmosphere had changed. Anderton was sitting by the big desk, clenching his fists and sweating; his whole posture telegraphed his controlled helplessness. Cheyney was bent over a seismograph, echo-sounding for the egg through the river bottom. If that even had a prayer of working, I knew, he'd have had the trains of the Hudson & Manhattan stopped; their rumbling course through their tubes would have blanked out any possible echo-pip from the egg.

"Wild goose chase?" Joan said, scanning my face.

"Not quite. I've got something, if I can just figure out what it is. Remember One-Shot Braun?"

"Yes. What's he got to do with it?"

"Nothing," I said. "But I want to bring him in. I don't think we'll lick this project before deadline without him."

"What good is a professional gambler on a job like this? He'll just get in the way."

I looked toward the television screen, which now showed an amorphous black mass, jutting up from a foundation of even deeper black. "Is that operation getting you anywhere?"

"Nothing's gotten us anywhere," Anderton interjected harshly. "We don't even know if that's the egg-the whole area is littered with crates. Harris, you've got to let me get that alert out!"

"Clark, how's the time going?"

Cheyney consulted the stopwatch. "Deadline in twenty-nine minutes," he said.

"All right, let's use those minutes. I'm beginning to see this thing a little clearer. Joan, what we've got here is a one-shot gamble; right?"

"In effect," she said cautiòusly.

"And it's my guess that we're never going to get the answer by diving for it-not in time, anyhow. Remember when the Navy lost a barge-load of shells in the harbor, back in '52? They scrabbled for them for a year and never pulled up a one; they finally had to warn the public that if it found anything funny-looking along the shore it shouldn't bang said object, or shake it either. We're better equipped than the Navy was then-but we're working against a deadline."

"If you'd admitted that earlier," Anderton said hoarsely, "we'd have half a million people out of the city by now. Maybe even a million."

"We haven't given up yet, colonel. The point is this, Joan: what we need is an inspired guess. Get anything from the prob series, Clark? I thought not. On a one-shot gamble of this kind, the 'laws' of chance are no good at all. For that matter, the so-called ESP experiments showed us long ago that even the way we construct random tables is full of holes-and that a man with a feeling for the essence of a gamble can make a monkey out of chance almost at will.

"And if there ever was such a man, Braun is it. That's why I asked him to come down here. I want him to look at that lump on the screen and-play a hunch."

"You're out of your mind," Anderton said.

A decorous knock spared me the trouble of having to deny, affirm or ignore the judgment. It was Braun; the messenger had been fast, and the gambler hadn't bothered to read what a college student had thought of him fifteen years ago. He came forward and held out his hand, while the others looked him over frankly.

He was impressive, all right. It would have been hard for a stranger to believe that he was aiming at respectability; to the eye, he was already there. He was tall and spare, and walked perfectly erect, not without spring despite his age. His clothing was as far from that of a gambler as you could have taken it by design: a black double-breasted suit with a thin vertical stripe, a gray silk tie with a pearl stickpin just barely large enough to be visible at all, a black Homburg; all perfectly fitted, all worn with proper casualness-one might almost say a formal casualness. It was only when he opened his mouth that One-Shot Braun was in the suit with him.

"I come over as soon as your runner got to me," he said. "What's the pitch, Andy?"

"Mr. Braun, this is Joan Hadamard, Clark Cheyney, Colonel Anderton. I'll be quick because we need speed now. A Polish ship has dropped something out in the harbor. We don't know what it is. It may be a hell-bomb, or it may be just somebody's old laundry. Obviously we've got to find out which-and we want you to tell us."

Braun's aristocratic eyebrows went up. "Me? Hell, Andy, I don't know nothing about things like that. I'm surprised with you. I thought CIA had all the brains it needed-ain't you got machines to tell you answers like that?"

I pointed silently to Joan, who had gone back to work the moment the introductions were over. She was still on the mike to the divers. She was saying: "What does it look like?"

"It's just a lump of something, Dr. Hadamard. Can't even tell its shape-it's buried too deeply in the mud." *Cloonk ... Oing, oing ...*

"Try the Geiger."

"We did. Nothing but background."

"Scintillation counter?"

"Nothing, Dr. Hadamard. Could be it's shielded."

"Let us do the guessing, Monig. All right, maybe it's got a clockwork fuse that didn't break with the impact. Or a gyroscopic fuse. Stick a stethoscope on it and see if you pick up a ticking or anything that sounds like a motor running."

There was a lag and I turned back to Braun. "As you can see, we're stymied. This is a long shot, Mr. Braun. One throw of the dice-one show-down hand. We've got to have an expert call it for us-somebody with a record of hits on long shots. That's why I called you."

"It's no good," he said. He took off the Homburg, took his handkerchief from his breast pocket, and wiped the hatband. "I can't do it."

"Why not?"

"It ain't my *kind* of thing," he said. "Look, I never in my life run odds on anything that made any difference. But this makes a difference. If I guess wrong —"

"Then we're all dead ducks. But why should you guess wrong? Your hunches have been working for sixty years now."

Braun wiped his face. "No. You don't get it. I wish you'd listen to me. Look, my wife and my kids are in the city. It ain't only my life, it's theirs, too. That's what I care about. That's why it's no good. On things that matter to me, *my hunches don't work.*"

I was stunned, and so, I could see, were Joan and Cheyney. I suppose I should have guessed it, but it had never occurred to me.

"Ten minutes," Cheyney said.

I looked up at Braun. He was frightened, and again I was surprised without having any right to be. I tried to keep at least my voice calm.

"Please try it anyhow, Mr. Braun-as a favor. It's already too late to do it any other way. And if you guess wrong, the outcome won't be any worse than if you don't try at all."

"My kids," he whispered. I don't think he knew that he was speaking aloud. I waited.

Then his eyes seemed to come back to the present. "All right," he said. "I told you the truth, Andy. Remember that. So-is it a bomb or ain't it? That's what's up for grabs, right?"

I nodded. He closed his eyes. An unexpected stab of pure fright went down my back. Without the eyes, Braun's face was a death mask.

The water sounds and the irregular ticking of a Geiger counter seemed to spring out from the audio speaker, four times as loud as before. I could even hear the pen of the seismograph scribbling away, until I looked at the instrument and saw that Clark had stopped it, probably long ago.

Droplets of sweat began to form along Braun's forehead and his upper lip. The handkerchief remained crushed in his hand.

Anderton said, "Of all the fool —"

"Hush!" Joan said quietly.

Slowly, Braun opened his eyes. "All right," he said. "You guys wanted it this way. *I say it's a bomb.*" He stared at us for a moment more-and then, all at once, the Timkin bearing burst. Words poured out of it. "Now you guys do something, do your job like I did mine-get my wife and kids out of there-empty the city-do something, *do something!*"

Anderton was already grabbing for the phone. "You're right, Mr. Braun. If it isn't already too late —"

Cheyney shot out a hand and caught Anderton's telephone arm by the wrist. "Wait a minute," he said.

"What d'you mean, 'wait a minute'? Haven't you already shot enough time?"

Cheyney did not let go; instead, he looked inquiringly at Joan and said, "One minute, Joan. You might as well go ahead."

She nodded and spoke into the mike. "Monig, unscrew the cap."

"Unscrew the cap?" the audio squawked. "But Dr. Hadamard, if that sets it off —"

"It won't go off. That's the one thing you can be sure it won't do."

"What is this?" Anderton demanded. "And what's this deadline stuff, anyhow?"

"The cap's off," Monig reported. "We're getting plenty of radiation now. Just a minute — Yeah. Dr. Hadamard, it's a bomb, all right. But it hasn't got a fuse. Now how could they have made a fool mistake like that?"

"In other words, it's a dud," Joan said.

"That's right, a dud."

Now, at last, Braun wiped his face, which was quite gray. "I told you the truth," he said grimly. "My hunches don't work on stuff like this."

"But they do," I said. "I'm sorry we put you through the wringer-and you too, colonel-but we couldn't let an opportunity like this slip. It was too good a chance for us to test how our facilities would stand up in a real bomb-drop."

"A real drop?" Anderton said. "Are you trying to say that CIA staged this? You ought to be shot, the whole pack of you!"

"No, not exactly," I said. "The enemy's responsible for the drop, all right. We got word last month from our man in Gdynia that they were going to do it, and that the bomb would be on board the *Ludmilla.* As I say, it was too good an opportunity to miss. We wanted to find out just how long it would take us to figure out the nature of the bomb-which we didn't know in detail-after it was dropped here. So we had our people in Gdynia defuse the thing after it was put on board the ship, but otherwise leave it entirely alone.

"Actually, you see, your hunch was right on the button as far as it went. We didn't ask you whether or not that object was a live bomb. We asked whether it was a bomb or not. You said it was, and you were right."

The expression on Braun's face was exactly like the one he had worn while he had been searching for his decision-except that, since his eyes were open, I could see that it was directed at me. "If this was the old days," he said in an ice-cold voice, "I might of made the colonel's idea come true. I don't go for tricks like this, Andy."

"It was more than a trick," Clark put in. "You'll remember we had a deadline on the test, Mr. Braun. Obviously, in a real drop we wouldn't have all the time in the world to figure out what kind of a thing had been dropped. If we had still failed to establish that when the deadline ran out, we would have had to allow evacuation of the city, with all the attendant risk that that was exactly what the enemy wanted us to do."

"So?"

"So we failed the test," I said. "At one minute short of the deadline, Joan had the divers unscrew the cap. In a real drop that would have resulted in a detonation, if the bomb was real; we'd never risk it. That we did do it in the test was a concession of failure-an admission that our usual methods didn't come through for us in time.

"And that means that you were the only person who did come through, Mr. Braun. If a real bomb-drop ever comes, we're going to have to have you here, as an active part of our investigation. Your intuition for the one-shot gamble was the one thing that bailed us out this time. Next time it may save eight million lives."

There was quite a long silence. All of us, Anderton included, watched Braun intently, but his impassive face failed to show any trace of how his thoughts were running.

When he did speak at last, what he said must have seemed insanely irrelevant to Anderton, and maybe to Cheyney too. And perhaps it meant nothing more to Joan than the final clinical note in a case history.

"It's funny," he said, "I was thinking of running for Congress next year from my district. But maybe this is more important."

It was, I believe, the sigh of a man at peace with himself.